Bu p s Soul

Inspirational Billionaire Romance

N. R. Emerald

Emerald Stone Publishing

Published by Emerald Stone Publishing

Print Book ISBN #: 978-976-97138-7-1

eBook ISBN #: 978-976-97138-6-4

Cover Design by Lynelle Caines, Lyn Elle Creative

Book Layout Using Atticus

Line edited by Cori Laatsch, Wisecracks & Paperbacks

Proofread by Suzanne Durant

DEDICATION

For The Reading Gems Facebook Group

Thank you for walking with me through a dark season.
Every post, comment, and emoji lifted my spirit.
I'm so grateful for this beautiful community.

Contents

One	1
Two	6
Three	10
Four	15
Five	21
Six	25
Seven	29
Eight	33
Nine	37
Ten	41
Eleven	47
Twelve	52
Thirteen	57

Fourteen	62
Fifteen	68
Sixteen	72
Seventeen	76
Eighteen	80
Nineteen	84
Twenty	89
Twenty-One	92
Twenty-Two	95
Twenty-Three	100
Twenty-Four	104
Twenty-Five	109
Twenty-Six	114
Twenty-Seven	117
Twenty-Eight	122
Twenty-Nine	125
Thirty	129
Thirty-One	134
Thirty-Two	139
Thirty-Three	142
Thirty-Four	147
Thirty-Five	151

Thirty-Six	156
Thirty-Seven	162
Thirty-Eight	166
Thirty-Nine	170
Forty	175
Forty-One	179
Forty-Two	184
Forty-Three	188
Forty-Four	192
Forty-Five	197
Forty-Six	200
Forty-Seven	204
Forty-Eight	209
Forty-Nine	213
Fifty	220
Fifty-One	224
Fifty-Two	229
Fifty-Three	233
Fifty-Four	236
Fifty-Five	241
Fifty-Six	246
Fifty-Seven	250

Fifty-Eight	256
Fifty-Nine	260
Sixty	263
Sixty-One	267
Sixty-Two	270
Epilogue	273
Blurb	282
From My Heart to Yours	283

One

Elena

This privilege we call life ... it can suck sometimes. And it really sucked right now.

I sat at Zoë's vanity, with its smooth marble top and gilded edges. What should I take with me? An unopened burgundy box adorned with rose-gold accents caught my eye, her favorite lipstick. Zoë's voice drifted through my mind, insisting that every woman should own at least one tube of Charlotte Tilbury's Matte Revolution. Turning the box over, I read the label: Red Carpet Red. Her bold red lips, perfectly matched to her olive skin and framed by jet-black curls, hovered in my memory. A color as vibrant and full of life as she was.

After grabbing the lipstick and a few other products, I dropped them into one of the cosmetic bags on her vanity. A spa day, just like when we were kids, was exactly what we needed. Her voice from years ago echoed in my mind, wrapping around me like a hug I hadn't realized I missed until now, the kind she gave when I first came home after being adopted. She comforted me, a little girl in a strange house, Nanna gone, everything unfamiliar. "You're my sister. We're your family." Back then, she was everything to me. Big sister. Role model.

My throat tightened and tears welled as I zipped the bag. Leaving her room, the pink hard hat on the shelf stopped me in my tracks. Dad always expected her to take over the business, especially as the lead electrical engineer. But we've come to terms with our new reality.

Yesterday, her further decline cut through me. Her head drooped, strength waning by the moment. Her lips, once lush and peachy, were cracked and parched. Dimmed eyes met mine, a faint flicker of recognition passing between us. Shared memories and the bond we built lingered in that fleeting connection, heavy with unspoken truths.

Her eyes carried the weight of understanding, the quiet acknowledgment of what neither of us dared to voice.

I wanted to make these last moments special.

For both of us.

I forced a smile. No tears. No tears, Elena. Only happy faces for Zoë. Straightening my back, I hurried down the corridor, one hand gripping the cosmetic bag and the other clutching the dress I bought from the boutique. She'd lost so much weight these past two months. Bathrobes had become her uniform. Not today. Today, I would get one of the nurses to help me dress her.

The door, usually closed, stood ajar. The bed empty.

They didn't mention more tests yesterday. They said there was nothing more they could do, that hospice care might be the next step. The cosmetic bag slipped from my grip as I turned and rushed to the nursing station.

"Nurse Paula!" My voice cracked as I approached her. "When will Zoë be back?"

She stepped around the desk, her hand resting on my shoulder. "Dr. Suleman asked to speak with you or your dad when you arrived."

A suffocating dread settled in my chest. "But where is my sister?"

Her lips tightened. "Dr. Suleman will explain." She led me back to Zoë's room. "Have a seat. One of the nurses has already called him."

I set the dress and bag on the sofa. My legs tensed, every muscle stiff with resistance. Sitting wasn't an option. I walked to the window. Buildings of staggering heights loomed, blocking the sea. Pressing my forehead against the glass, I wrapped my arms around myself, the chill of the AC raising bumps along my skin. My stomach churned as a hollow ache of anxiety twisted through me.

A rush of cool air brushed against my back. Light spilled into the room as footsteps entered. Turning, I met Dr. Suleman's gaze. His hands rested in his pockets, his face unreadable but grave.

"Ms. Callos," he began, voice soft. "I'm sorry. Zoë died early this morning."

The words didn't register. "What?" My chest tightened, my voice trembled.

My arms dropped to my sides, hands shaking uncontrollably. "Why didn't anyone call us?"

His hands came up in a placating gesture. "She wanted it this way."

"No. No. Nooo," escaped my lips. "She wouldn't. She would have wanted us here with her." A tear broke free, slipping down my cheek. "I wanted to be here with her." Taking a deep breath and steadying myself, I said firmly, "Dad... wanted to be here."

Dr. Suleman, clad in gray, seemed to embody the colorless world around me. "I want to see her," I whispered.

He took a step forward, and I stepped back, as if distance could shield me from the weight of his words.

"There's more," he said in a heavy voice.

"More?"

He nodded. His gaze shifted, no longer meeting mine. The sick feeling spread, pooling in my stomach. As he opened his mouth and spoke, each word cut like an axe, the final blow shattering my heart into a million pieces.

It didn't make sense. None of it made sense. Zoë wouldn't have ...

She couldn't have ...

Two

Bishop

Ten months ago, Danielle's voice bubbled with excitement over the phone. "Gavin and I are having a baby," she announced, almost breathless. She planned to take six months off for maternity leave, and before she could even ask, I assured her I would oversee the foundation. How could I say no? Danielle was my sister's best friend, the one who stood by her through everything, right until the end. She was right there with us, helping set up the Anaís Hope Foundation. After her death, Danielle took over as director, pouring every ounce of herself into the work my sister left behind.

The foundation gave me a shift I hadn't known I needed. After years of planning and executing covert missions, I had been running on fumes. When I mentioned to Drago that I would cut back on fieldwork for a few months, I didn't realize just how badly I needed a break. The relentless grind of building

BI International into a security powerhouse consumed all my time and energy. And the work we did for governments and organizations, the kind that could never go on the books, only added to the weight pressing down on me.

I glanced down at my watch. Three more hours. The number glared back at me from the watch face as the elevator doors slid shut. Four more hours until Melinda. Her **GentlemanClub** status said she was up for some fun tonight. Fun and maybe a little more than fun. Three days since my last hookup. The itch in my pants was impossible to ignore. The perplexing thing was, since being here at the foundation full time now for about four weeks, my need for sex became more necessary but less fulfilling. Although I welcomed the break from work, maybe there is still some part of me that missed it all.

I'm either a certified workaholic or an adrenaline junkie.

Maybe both.

I leaned in to press the button to lock the elevator, ensuring no one else could get on with me. As the doors slid to close, a hand shot through the gap, followed by another to hold them open. A woman stepped inside with her phone glued to her ear. She didn't even glance my way. Great. Now I had to listen to her for the next few seconds. Thank God these lifts moved fast. Please don't let them stop before reaching the top floor.

My luck ran out. The elevator jolted to a stop on the next floor, but whoever called it must've changed their mind. The doors slid shut again, and the woman's voice filled the small space.

"No, Dad," she said, her tone sharp yet edged with worry. She shifted her weight, her body practically humming with tension. "Yes, I called our attorney, but they're the ones who suggested contacting the Anaís Hope Foundation. They think their attorneys might be able to figure out if this is even legal."

She glanced at the numbers lighting up above the doors, her fingers twitching against the phone. "Dad, it doesn't add up. Zoë wouldn't agree to cremation without saying a word to me. We always talked about a funeral and a burial." She paused. "I was her health surrogate. Or at least, I thought I was until today. Turns out she wanted to make all her own decisions."

Her voice cracked on the last word, and she tipped her head back, eyes locking on the ceiling as if it held the answers. Then, as if feeling my gaze, she turned toward me.

Even with her pink-stained eyes and weariness etched across her face, she was stunning. Absolutely stunning. Her lower lip quivered before she pressed it flat, like she was trying to seal in whatever might come spilling out. Grief clung to her, but somehow, it only made her more unforgettable.

Her eyes scanned me, slowly and deliberately, traveling from my shoes up to my tie. The elevator dinged as it reached another floor, but this time, the doors didn't open.

"By any chance, are you an attorney?" she asked, her voice a mix of hope and resignation.

"Do I look like an attorney?"

She wrinkled her forehead. Like to say, *Idiot, I wouldn't ask unless I thought you were.* "The way you're dressed, either an attorney or an investment banker. But I'm really hoping for the former."

"Sorry to disappoint," I said. "Neither."

She sighed and her shoulders sank as she turned back to her phone. "Sorry, Dad. I thought I found someone who could help, but no luck." Her voice softened, carrying the exhaustion that came from chasing answers and hitting walls. "I don't know. He's probably here to donate or something." She hesitated, her fingers brushing the edge of her phone.

"Anyway, I'm getting out now. But Dad, I promise I will do everything in my power to make sure Zoë gets a proper burial."

She lifted her face to the ceiling again, her lips moving silently, almost like a prayer.

As if pleading.

Hoping.

Something stirred in me as I watched her. And for once, it wasn't lust.

What my green-eyed intruder didn't know is I'm no attorney ... but maybe, just maybe, I'm the miracle she needs.

Three

Elena

The gentleman in the tailored navy-blue suit gestured as the elevator doors slid open, a silent, courteous, *Ladies first.* A sad smile tugged at my lips. Zoë would've spotted the designer instantly, probably rattling off details about the cut and fabric like it was second nature. She should have been a designer, not an electrical engineer.

Stepping out of the elevator, I tucked my phone into my bag. Dropping it now wasn't an option. My palms were clammy, and the faint buzz of anxiety pressed at my ribs. The gentleman stepped out behind me, but when I glanced up, he had disappeared.

I wanted to ask him for directions, but it didn't matter. A pale-green wall ahead pointed to the reception area. I glanced at my watch, 3:36 p.m. Still some time before they closed. Hopefully enough for them to do something. *Anything.*

Adjusting the strap of my bag, I moved toward the reception area. Rounding the corner, I froze. The space looked more like a luxury hotel lobby than an office. Oversized navy armchairs flanked antique, pink-upholstered chairs, and a crystal chandelier cast rainbows of light across the room.

A slow breath escaped my lips. At least they care about appearances.

A woman in a bright-yellow wrap dress stood from a sleek desk and walked toward me, hand extended. "I'm Helene. Welcome. How can we assist you?"

God, please let them be able to help.

"I need to speak with an attorney. My sister …" The words crumbled in my throat, composure slipping. My grip tightened around her hand, the connection grounding me.

"An attorney," I whispered. "I understand you have attorneys here. Who can help."

Her expression softened. "Have a seat, dear. Let me see when we can schedule you."

"No." My head shook before the word left my lips, my fingers still clinging to her hand. "You don't understand. I need someone today."

Her steady grip anchored me, firm but kind. "Let me check."

She stepped back to her desk, retrieving a tablet in a cover that matched the walls. "If we can't see you today, I'll try to schedule you for first thing tomorrow. In the meantime, please fill this out. The more details you provide, the better we'll be able to assist."

The tablet was heavy in my hands, which trembled as I typed. Each word pulled me deeper into the gravity of why I was here. Zoë's name. My name. Details I didn't want to think about but couldn't avoid. If they asked for my bank information, I might've handed that over too.

When I finished, Helene was on a call, so I left the tablet on her desk and wandered around the room. Two women sat together on a sofa. The older one held some documents while the younger, frail but determined, typed away on the tablet. That kind of frailty often came with a quiet but unrelenting strength, the kind born from a fight to live.

My gaze landed on a photo display of some women. Not models. Except for the vibrant reds, greens, and blues of their gowns, the image was black and white. The colors leapt off the picture. The women wore smiles of victory.

"That picture stops me every time too."

I jumped, not having heard anyone approach.

"Sorry, didn't mean to scare you."

"No, it's fine." I turned back to the display. "I see strength and triumph."

The woman beside me wore a black pantsuit paired with a gray sheer blouse. Her sleek black hair was pulled into a high ponytail. Standing next to me, I guessed she was about five foot two.

"Some women in that picture," she explained, "had beaten cancer. Others knew they were dying. But all of them were victorious. They faced their demons and conquered." She traced the edge of the frame. "The picture is called 'Victory Through Grace.'" Removing her hand from the frame, she turned towards me. "Ms. Callos, I'm Camila, one of the attorneys with the foundation."

Some people might underestimate her, this petite woman in a sharp suit with a soft voice. But not me. As a female electrical project manager, I walked into meetings where clients assumed I was my father's assistant, not the project manager. They would direct their questions to whichever male accompanied me to the meeting. Often, I had to interject to set them straight.

"Follow me. This way."

I followed Camila into a room that continued the pale-green theme, furnished with six chairs around a table set with a tray for coffee and tea.

"Have a seat." She slipped a recorder from her jacket pocket. "I glanced at your notes, but I would like you to tell me your account."

"Okay." I nodded. Her assuredness and warmth loosened the knot in my stomach.

"Mind if I record?"

I removed the messenger bag draped across my chest and rested it on the chair beside me. "Not at all."

Just as Camila was about to press record, the soft whisper of a door gliding open behind me drew my attention. Her brow arched as she turned slightly. "You're joining us?"

A voice answered, a low timbre that rolled over me, warm and unhurried. Heat prickled along the back of my neck, and I sat up straighter without thinking.

"I'll sit in on this one."

My brows furrowed as the gentleman from the elevator slid into the chair opposite me.

Four

Bishop

Lifting the door handle, I slid into the car. The story Elena shared with Camila and me sounded nothing like St. Andrews Hospital. We had partnered with them for over five years, ever since Anaís was diagnosed. I pulled out of the parking lot and tapped the voice button on the steering wheel, "Call Nathan Carmichael."

The call barely rang before Nathan's professional, yet light tone, greeted me. "Alejandro Bishop, to what do I owe the pleasure, my friend? If you're calling to offer us money, you know I'm always happy to help you single, unmarried billionaires spend it, especially for a good cause."

"Nathan, I'm always willing to take one for the team. Somebody's gotta be rich and lonely, and that's me."

"It doesn't have to be that way, my friend. I have two younger sisters who practically drool over you. I still can't figure out why."

"Summer and Angelina have always had better taste than you," I retorted, smirking.

"Knowing you, this isn't a social call. What's going on?"

"Camila, one of our attorneys. You might've worked with her."

"Yes, I know her. She helped our team secure funding last year for the new cancer research wing. You know we would pull out all the stops for her."

"I'm hoping that's the case because she'll be reaching out, not for herself, but on behalf of someone she's advocating for. A young woman visited the foundation today after being informed her sister died earlier this morning. No one from the hospital contacted the family, and now she's being told her sister requested cremation and only her ashes will be released to the family."

"Who's the patient?"

"Zoë Callos."

"I'll look into it. But I'll tell you this. Recently, several younger patients, being so environmentally conscious, have been opting for cremation. They also want to spare their families the grief of a funeral and transition with dignity. Even if a family member wasn't there, you can be sure our medical team took care of things properly. I'll dig into it for you."

"Thanks, man."

"No problem. While I'm holed up in my office at seven o'clock, I bet you're out there breaking some lady's heart."

"You sure it isn't mine that's breaking?" For a second, Liliana flashed through my mind. She was unzipping her black cocktail dress, crawling across the floor to her very married boss like she was in some low-budget porn movie.

I shook my head. She didn't deserve a square foot of space in my thoughts.

"Nathan, this is all part of my public service," I said, voice dry. "Like I told you, always willing to take one for the team." I smirked, eyes on the road as brake lights flared in front of me. "You family men can't have your cake and eat it too. I'm eating all the cake for you."

Nathan chuckled a reply. "Be careful. All that cake isn't good for you." His voice crackled through the phone as he ended the call.

The valet approached as I opened the door. "Bishop, how are you, sir?"

"Rico. Good, man. How is married life? Six months now, right?"

Rico responded with a nod and said, "Great! We have a baby on the way."

I clapped him on the shoulder, eyes widening, "Congrats, man! You'll be a fine dad."

He beamed. "Thanks, sir."

The young man's face lit up brighter than any spotlight in a club. Twelve months ago, Liliana made it crystal clear that kind of life with the ring, the vows, and the forever was for guys like Rico.

Not me.

Definitely not me.

My phone buzzed in my hand, confirming my date's arrival. Did they do this for all their guests, or was it because of my long-term room rental? If it was the latter, I should've cared ... but shame and I parted ways long ago. No point pretending. The staff knew exactly what these were. Hookups.

When I stepped into the bar, the air hit me first, a heady mix of aged rum, subtle hints of designer perfume, and the crisp, clean scent of polished mahogany counters. Voices layered over one another, punctuated by bursts of laughter and the occasional clink of glasses. The hum of conversation created a low, steady rhythm that matched the soft jazz spilling from hidden speakers. For a Tuesday night, the place was alive. Couples leaned close in shadowed corners, a group of suits argued over a bill near the bar, and the faint glow of phones lit up faces at scattered tables.

A familiar server approached, his smile practiced but sharp. "Good evening, sir. Green dress. Hair in a high ponytail," he said, nodding toward the back.

I slipped him a fifty, and he pocketed it with ease. "Thanks, man."

As I walked over, her eyes lifted to mine. She tossed her long, sleek hair over her right shoulder, angled her head, and smiled, a slow, practiced curve of her lips that was equal parts seduction and challenge. It was the kind of smile that used to light me up. Now, it barely registered. The buzz, the high I used to get as I moved in on my date, was missing.

There was nothing wrong with her. Focus, Bishop. Get your head in the game. I ran my eyes over her. The dress hugged every curve, her breasts looked one shift away from spilling out of her provocatively low V-cut blouse, and I had no doubt the hem stopped below her butt when she stood.

I shook my head, remembering a woman last month who told me panties weren't mean to be worn with some dresses. "And I only wear those ones," she said with a wink.

Melinda was stunning. Golden skin. Long legs. A face that could tempt a saint. But ... No buts. Tonight was about scratching an itch.

When I reached her, I leaned in and kissed her cheek. "You're even more beautiful in person."

She batted her lashes at me. Fake. As fake as a thousand-dollar bill. They nearly poked me in the eye.

"Let's go up to my room," I said right away, grabbing her hand.

She batted those lashes again. "Aren't we having dinner?"

I guided her off the stool, steadying her to make sure she didn't topple over in those sky-high heels. I had no doubt they could double as weapons.

"Of course," I said smoothly. "The chef prepared a nice spread for us in the room. You did say you were up for fun."

"Bishop, I'm up for more than fun." Her hand brushed against the zipper of my pants.

Five

Bishop

Buzzing.

Blinking a few times before my eyes opened.

A head rested on my chest. A leg wrapped around mine.

More buzzing.

Champagne fogged my mind. I had two bottles last night, just to get me in the right headspace. I untangled myself from Melinda, who apparently fused herself to me during the night, and reached for my phone.

I stepped over two condom wrappers as I answered. "Yeah?"

Camila's voice slid through the line like syrup, thick with amusement. "Disturbing you, lover boy?"

"Remind me why I haven't fired you yet," I shot back, rubbing the ache at the back of my neck.

"Because you can't."

The clock on my phone read 5:56 a.m. Outside, it was still dark. "I spoke with Nathan last night. He promised to look into it."

"That's why I'm calling. He sent me the paperwork. I pored over the documents. It's rock solid."

"Send it to me. Let me take a look."

"Will do. I wish I could've done more," she said before pausing. "Want me to call Elena?"

I opened the drapes. Darkness still clung to the horizon. Fitting for the moment. "No. Let me review what you've got first."

"There's nothing there."

"I'll look," I snapped, running a hand through my hair. I stared out the window for a moment. "Listening to her … it reminded me of the bond Anaís and I shared."

"Bishop, you're getting sentimental in your old age."

"Remind me to speak to Danielle about your insubordination when she's back."

Camila's laugh echoed through the phone. Behind me, soft footsteps entered the living room. Hands wrapped around me, and tiny bites pressed along the center of my back.

"Camila, we'll talk later."

"Sure, lover boy." She hung up.

Melinda's voice purred behind me. "Coming back to bed?"

Turning, I said, "As much as I'd love to, I've got files to review."

Wrapping the sheet around us and batting her lashes, she teased, "Why do I feel like you're a love-them-and-leave-them type? If that's the case, I want more of this glorious body of yours."

She tugged me toward her with the sheet.

She leaned in, aiming for a kiss on my lips. I turned away. No kissing. Too intimate. My inner voice scolded me. Kissing was off limits, but sex wasn't?

"As tempting as your offer is, let's shower and order breakfast."

"The showering part sounds even better."

"You go ahead. I'll arrange room service."

Her pout said everything.

She wasn't wrong. I never did repeats.

She padded back to the bedroom, and I stood there as the morning light began to creep through the windows. I reflected on last night. It took nearly two bottles of champagne to get me to sleep with her. Gosh, the woman was beautiful. But after we ate, my conscience niggled at me. An orchestrated setup for sex.

Not love. Just sex.

My conscience chose the worst possible time to show up.

Two bottles of champagne. Which I drank most of. Melinda was not much of a drinker, and she was also not about wasting time. The girl knew what she wanted.

The phone buzzed in my hand, dragging me out of my thoughts. I slipped on a robe, ordered room service, and sat on the sofa to review the documents Camila sent.

Glancing at the email, I knew this might be the first time in years I had to disappoint a woman. And I didn't want to.

Six

Elena

"Imani, Dad called, and he's walking over—"

The doorbell sang a single, breathy flute note, drawn out like the last exhale of a ghost. It drifted through the room, eerie and weightless, a stark contrast to the heaviness pressing against my ribs, making it hard to breathe.

Maybe it wasn't the room. Maybe it was me. The weight of Zoë. The weight of responsibility.

God, let me do right by her. Please.

Imani opened the door and wrapped Dad in a hug. "Theo. Since Elena called, know that I've been praying."

She loomed over him, her 5′11″ frame forcing his head to tilt back as he met her gaze. If the moment had been different, the sight might have drawn a laugh, her height swallowing his by a solid four inches, his stance shifting like he was used to compensating for it. But nothing about this was funny.

"Imani brought over her famous spinach and jerk chicken quiche for you."

I lifted my gaze to Imani, hoping she could see the gratitude I couldn't voice. Her being here meant more than I could say.

The last thing I wanted to do was eat. But this wasn't about me. This was about making sure *he* ate. That we did.

After leaving the foundation, I rushed home to be with Dad, only he wasn't there. And there was only one other place he could have been. My chest tightened as I walked to Zoë's house.

There he was.

Standing.

Staring.

Lost in space and in his mind. I rested my head on his shoulder.

"The hospice project," Dad's voice caught. "She wanted it. We never expected her to go so fast. The new treatment was supposed to slow the cancer. But it didn't." His voice broke. "Elena, she's gone. They're gone. She's with her mom now. They both left me. It's me and you now. They left us." He swallowed hard. "I wanted that project for her. It was the only thing she ever asked about when I visited, if we heard any news on our tender. That was the last proposal she worked on."

Silence settled between us, thick with everything we couldn't say.

My eyes scanned the room, clinging to the remnants of her. The bright yellow accent wall, her signature burst of sunshine. The collage of framed selfies, moments she captured, never knowing they would become our lifeline to her. Did she have any inkling when she left this place two weeks ago that it would be for the last time?

My heart ached with the thought.

We hoped.

The doctors hoped.

Dad kissed my forehead. "Go home. I'll stay here for a few minutes."

Leaving him, I stood vigil by my window, watching. He stayed for hours, eventually leaving just before midnight.

I didn't even know how to hold it all together.

Dad.

The company.

Waiting for someone to tell me when I can even bury my sister.

Imani led Dad to the table while I returned to the kitchen to get the pot of tea for Dad and Imani and a strong black coffee for me. Between keeping an eye on Dad last night and tossing and turning from worry, I was running on fumes. Knowing Zoë was finally out of her pain should have brought some comfort, except for how it all unfolded. Zoë always said, *"God will heal me someday, either this side of heaven or the other."*

Flute notes drifted through the kitchen. The gate. Someone had to be at the entrance. Only four properties sat inside our family's gated community, and everyone was already here.

Well, except for my brother. Zen lived in Etim now. He already called, restless, wanting to leave, but I told him we should know something by today. Hopefully.

If we didn't ... I knew Zen would come home and turn the world upside down to get answers. Subtlety had never been his strength. His CEO, in-charge personality meant he bulldozed through problems. But diplomacy? Not his thing. His approach in this situation might make things worse.

Voices drifted into the kitchen. Zen's voice was deep, but this one sounded different.

Definitely not Zen.

Seven

Bishop

A tall, elegant woman in blue jeans and a light blue button-down shirt opened the door. "Come in. Elena told us about you and your foundation."

"Sorry for dropping by unannounced."

"Nonsense. When you buzzed the gate and said who you were, I silently thanked God. Elena will be glad to see you. She's trying to hold it together, but I hope you can give her some hope. I'm Imani."

I shook the extended hand.

I doubted my news would bring them anything close to hope or peace.

Acceptance.

That was what they needed. Sometimes, we don't know what our loved ones are thinking when they know they're going to die. Zoë, though I never met her, would have put her family first in her own way.

"Join us for breakfast. Elena will be right out."

"I'll just have a cup of coffee." I protested. "Already ate."

The living room was painted a soft gray. Angled in the corner sat an oversized lavender chair, probably meant for one but big enough for two, maybe three. It was the only pop of color in the room, pulling the eye the moment I stepped in.

Past the chair, my gaze drifted, then stopped. My breath hitched. My heart pounded, the rhythm fast and sharp, as if it were dancing the rumba in appreciation of the masterpiece displayed on the wall.

It was an oil painting. A woman dressed in a black gown, and a flute poised at her lips. Her eyes were closed, lost in the music. The tilt of her head, the curve of her fingers, the way the painter captured her ... I could see her, hear her. As if I were there, caught in the moment with her.

If it had a price tag, I would have reached for my wallet. Some things don't just hang on a wall.

They breathe.

This painting breathed.

"Beautiful, isn't it?"

I turned.

"That's Elena's last performance with the orchestra. She stopped." A wistful smile curved Imani's lips, one that never quite reached her eyes. "Never said why she stopped playing. Maybe to focus more on the family business." She tilted her head, studying the painting. “So talented. A gift to be shared, not hidden.”

Imani’s voice held a quiet reverence. Her expression shifted, soft with pride but shadowed by something unspoken. Regret. Loss.

“That’s Elena?” My gaze drifted back to the painting.

So different.

Very different.

Definitely different from the woman I met yesterday. Black jeans, a plain black T-shirt. If not for the well-worn leather messenger bag, which cost a few hundred dollars, I would have figured she was one paycheck away from being homeless.

“Let me introduce you. Theo, this is Alejandro Bishop.”

A man with salt-and-pepper hair and red-rimmed eyes stood and shook my hand. “Thank you. Elena told me you’re looking into everything. All we want is to give her a proper homegoing service.”

Homegoing service?

They sounded like my parents. Like Anaís. Churchgoers, at the very least.

“My deepest condolences, sir.”

“Drop the ‘sir.’ Theo is just fine.”

I turned to Imani. Elegant. A beautiful golden complexion with a fashionably slanted bob, short in the back, long in the front.

What was her connection to Theo? Girlfriend? Fiancée?

From the form Elena completed yesterday, I knew his wife died fifteen years ago. I'd bet on fiancée. Though there was no ring on her finger.

Their eyes stayed on mine. My chest tightened.

Why do I care?

Five minutes ago, I didn't even know these people. Less than twenty-four hours ago, I didn't even know Elena.

God, I hated what I had to tell them.

A sharp gasp cut through the room. My gaze snapped toward the sound.

Eight

Elena

Balancing a tray with tea, coffee, and mugs, I rounded the corner and stopped.

Alejandro Bishop.

My mouth opened. A sound escaped.

Same blue suit. Less crisp than yesterday. My eyebrows furrowed for a moment. He never made it home.

His gaze locked on to mine. A pause. Heavy. Unreadable.

It took the strength of Hercules to keep the tray steady. Pushing forward, I set it gently down on the dining room table.

"Any news?" The words rushed out before I could stop them.

"Alejandro is going to have coffee," Imani offered.

"Sorry. My manners," I muttered.

His dark eyes stayed on mine. Steady. His brows pulled together, just a fraction. He took a slow inhale, then his jaw tensed.

Although he was on the other side of the table, his gaze mirrored concern.

Even compassion.

Everything he wanted to say but couldn't.

At least, that's what I thought. Then again, I didn't know this man. This man now walking around the table to sit next to me, still wearing the same suit from yesterday.

"Let's sit and hear what the young man has to say," Dad suggested.

"Theo is right. Let's sit, have something to eat, then we can talk afterward."

"Imani, Alejandro may have somewhere to be," I said, shifting my eyes toward him.

"I'm certain it will still be there in thirty minutes," she replied smoothly. "He can have a cup of coffee and one of my famous quiches."

"Whatever you say," Alejandro conceded, his deep, Latin-accented voice wrapping around the words.

With that settled, I held out my hand. His brows shot up. Across the table, Dad and Imani's hands were already linked. Imani stretched across and took Alejandro's hand. I took Dad's.

Dad blessed the breakfast and prayed, for strength, for whatever we would face as a family.

Alejandro's grip tightened. If Dad continued any longer, my fingers would be bruised.

I thanked God when Dad said amen.

Even given the circumstances, this was turning into one odd morning.

Imani ... being Imani. Bossing a billionaire around. Always in control.

Dad, usually the one asking if I met a nice guy at church and always pointing out members he thought would be a good fit for me, yet here he was, welcoming a man who obviously came straight from a hookup last night with open arms.

"This quiche is different. I love the hint of pepper. Just the right balance."

Imani blushed.

Imani *doesn't* blush.

I rolled my eyes discreetly.

Yup. He was all charm.

I set down my fork. Dad only took a few bites of his quiche but at least ate his salad. My plate remained untouched. Two cups of coffee in, I couldn't wait any longer.

"So, what did you find?"

Silence descended over the room. Forks stilled. Mugs, held mid-air, lowered back to the table.

Alejandro placed his cup down. "Camila, the attorney you met yesterday, spoke with the hospital's CEO. We got access to Zoë's records. We both reviewed them."

He bowed his head for a moment, then lifted it again, his gaze shifting from Imani, to Dad, then me.

"And?" I asked.

"The hospital was only following Zoë's request."

We wouldn't see her face again. Not one more time.

A hollow ache spread through my chest. Breathe. I forced in air, but it barely reached my lungs. My throat tightened. My eyes burned. Don't break. Not now.

Across the table, Imani reached for Dad's hand. Held on. Clung. As if letting go would make it real.

"So there's nothing we can do?" My voice was barely above a whisper.

His hand brushed mine. Warm. Steady. A quiet anchor in the storm. A fleeting touch, yet it set off something in me I didn't want to acknowledge.

"Yes, there is." His voice was low, certain. "There is something you can do."

Nine

Bishop

"Onika, we're short by 1.5 million dollars for this year's gala."

"I'm working my magic," Onika replied, one hand on her hip and the other sweeping toward the sleek, glossy black conference table that dominated the boardroom. The polished surface reflected the city skyline through the floor-to-ceiling windows. Six other planning team members sat around it, waiting. "Any ideas? Seeing Bishop wants to raise our hospital donation to five million."

"Five million?" Camila's brow arched.

"Nathan Carmichael called yesterday," I said. "Their groundbreaking research needs continued funding, and they're looking for donors. I want us to contribute two million this year. Suggestions?"

"Besides you personally covering the shortfall?" someone quipped from near the door.

"I have a suggestion," the newest team member said, leaning forward. We recruited Wesley from one of New York's top marketing firms. He jumped at the chance to relocate for less cold and more sunshine. He took a sip of water before continuing. "What if we host a cocktail event that same evening? Invite the CEOs we're targeting, give them a virtual experience around the research. We could easily exceed the goal."

Turning to Onika, I asked, "Can we make it happen?"

She smirked, tapping a manicured finger against the table. "Give me two days, and with Wesley's help, I'm certain we can pull it off."

"Great job, team. Wesley, good idea."

"Just doing my job, boss."

The others trickled out, but I stayed seated.

Could I ever do enough? Raise enough?

Camila slipped into the chair next to mine. "Your sister would be proud of what you've built. How you've continued her legacy."

I leaned back, staring at the ceiling. "Thanks."

Eight days. Three hours. Five minutes.

That's how long it had been since I told Elena about her sister.

Donating money from a distance was one thing. Sitting at a family's dinner table delivering news they didn't want to hear was another.

"Are you going to the memorial service?"

She didn't need to say the name. Through Nathan, I kept tabs on the family.

"Are you?"

"Can't. My sister's having dental surgery, and I've been assigned chauffeur duty. How about you?"

I scrubbed a hand over my mouth and exhaled before saying, "No. On this, I'm sticking to our philosophy. We care. We support. But more importantly, we know when our role ends."

Her eyes narrowed. "Our role is over. But is yours?"

I lifted a brow.

"Don't look at me like that." She folded her arms. "All of a sudden you're increasing the donation to the hospital? And we both know Elena's sister was part of this trial."

My phone vibrated against the table. I picked it up but hesitated before checking the message.

"This is what we do, Camila. We help."

"If you say so." She stood up, pushing her chair away from the table, and paused at the door. "Enjoy your evening."

The door clicked shut.

I glanced at my screen.

GentlemanClub: Date with Roxanne confirmed.

Every damn minute since leaving Elena Callos and her family, I hadn't been able to shake them. Each time I attempted to schedule a date, I hesitated.

But life moves on.

My life moves on.

The date was at seven. The clock read three.

Three o'clock.

Eight days. Four hours. One minute.

The second hand dragged forward, mocking me from the wall.

Alejandro Bishop ... YOUR JOB IS DONE.

I grabbed my phone.

Why the hell was I even lying to myself?

Roxanne.

Think Roxanne.

Ten

Bishop

Slipping into the last row near the door, I took in the crowd of over three hundred people. The ushers had done a good job filling the church from the front. No wooden pews here, just cushioned chairs arranged in neat rows, divided by two aisles. Only a few seats in the back remained empty.

Pulling this kind of attendance for a memorial service on a weekday said a lot about Zoë.

Again, why was I even here?

Camila got in my head.

Guilt.

Yeah, guilt.

Days passed, but the image of Elena's green eyes, heavy with unshed tears, stayed with me. When I told her, "You can do something. Accept Zoë's wishes," it wasn't what she wanted to hear. None of them wanted to hear it. But there was nothing more that could have been done.

The pastor, an older version of that Outlander actor, Sam Heughan, announced, "We will close this Thanksgiving Service for the life of Zoë Callos with a tribute from her sister, Elena."

My gaze shifted to the monitor overhead as she stepped onto the platform. High heels. White flowing pants. A matching cap-sleeve top that showed off toned arms. When she turned, red lipstick, bold and sinful, stood out against her warm, bronzed skin.

Lips that begged to be kissed until the world faded. I clenched my jaw. I shouldn't have been looking at her lips, not here, not now, but they made my mouth dry.

Seeing Elena sent a jolt to my system ... like missing a step on solid ground. It hit low in my chest, sharp and unexpected, making my breath hitch before I got it under control.

Elena Callos ... was breathtaking.

Should I even have these thoughts at a memorial service?

Or at all?

She stepped toward the microphone. "Zoë always said a lady should have a red lipstick in her arsenal. If you knew her, red lipstick was her signature look." She exhaled, then added, "This was one of her favorite songs. You can follow the words on the screen."

Imani joined her on the keyboard. These women were gifted.

The song title flashed across the screen: "I Can Only Imagine" – MercyMe.

Lyrics filled the display, but my focus stayed on Elena. The moment she raised the flute to her lips, something twisted inside me. I itched to pull out my phone, to capture her like some fool with a schoolboy crush.

Full lips, the kind that dipped at the center and curved like they knew how to ruin a man. What would I give to be that flute now?

The chords flowed through the church, wrapping around me, pulling me under.

Applause broke the spell. She turned to leave the platform, and I stood to take my exit. Respects paid. Duty done.

Whatever that was, it stayed here. I had other things to handle, like Roxanne.

As I gazed out my bedroom window, the empty cognac glass sat heavy in my palm. Where was the excitement for tonight?

I tore out of the church parking lot like demons chased me. Well, they were, my demons. All the way home, soft, breathy notes floated in my head.

Red lips. Green eyes.

They still haunted me.

Showering and changing out of my suit into jeans and a leather jacket should've shifted my mood as I got ready for my hook-up. But on the drive from home to the hotel, my mind kept pulling me back to Elena.

Get out of your head, Bishop.

It's just guilt ... mixed with a touch of lust. You don't know the girl ... or her family.

Move on.

I arrived early and opted to have another drink in my guest room, still trying to shake the day. The phone vibrated on the table behind me. Roxanne had arrived. Turning, I walked to the bar and poured another shot of brandy, my third for the evening, before heading downstairs.

It had been over a week since Melinda.

I needed this.

My mind needed this.

And really, my body needed to release all this tension.

Tossing back the brandy, I grabbed the key card and left. Roxanne sat at the bar, where the staff always placed my women while they waited for me. Petite, blonde, red dress. Her profile said she was twenty-five and had recently moved to the area. She wanted safe fun, no commitment. Jackpot.

Sliding onto the stool next to her, I said, "I'm Bishop."

She smiled. "You're even more handsome in person."

"Shouldn't that be my line?"

"You find me handsome?" She arched a brow.

"Ready for dinner?"

"Dinner. Is that code for something else?" She ran her eyes up and down me, her broad smile teasing. "I'm fine skipping dinner. When I said I was up for fun," she trailed her manicured fingers down my arm, "I meant it."

"Let's have dinner."

"You know, I ate before coming here, but I could have an appetizer," she offered.

Why was I even bothering with dinner in the restaurant? We could eat in the room. Not that eating was usually what happened.

Resting my hand on her back, I said, "Let me order room service then. At least I can get something to eat."

She smiled.

We went up to the room, and I opened the door and let her in. As soon as it clicked shut, she stepped forward in her high heels, her dress barely covering her behind. Her fingers reached for the hem, then she pulled it over her head.

Roxanne stood there, looking like the girl-next-door version of a porn star, wrapped in a red, lace strapless bra and matching panties.

"Don't you find me attractive?"

Something in me stalled. "Something's telling me this isn't really your thing."

I didn't even know why I cared. She was offering herself to me.

"This wasn't me until last week. Until I caught my fiancé with my best friend." She reached behind her back to unhook her bra. "To hell with being faithful. To hell with relationships and commitments. I just want to have fun."

The bra hit the floor. She sauntered toward me, swaying her hips. I fully understood how she felt. Liliana and I weren't even engaged, and her betrayal cut deep. But this path I started on ...

She threw her arms around my neck. "Let's have fun. Make me forget." Her brown eyes, warm like honey, stared into mine. Her soft, full breasts pressed against my chest.

I sighed and reached for the hands she wrapped around my neck. "Roxanne. Trust me. You don't forget."

Eleven

Elena

The sharp tang of fresh paint clung to the air, mixing with the low, constant hum of electricity coursing through newly laid circuits. Three team members sat around the polished oak table, their faces reflecting both pride and exhaustion. One seat remained empty.

Forever empty.

Two months since Zoë's passing.

"Boss. Elena. We did it!" Luis shouted, his grin wide. But his glance flickered, just for a second, toward that vacant chair to my right. Zoë's spot. We always sat next to each other. She often led the final handover.

The twenty-two-room hotel, with its sleek, modern touches, catered to executives with money to burn. It was set to open in two days. Standard rooms were priced at eight hundred a night, though nothing about them was standard.

"Let's do one final walkthrough." The words scraped against the knot in my throat. "Sophie, are the occupancy sensors calibrated? The hotel director said the delay in shutting off was too long. We wanted it down to two minutes."

"Yes. It's exactly two minutes."

"Good." A slow exhale. "We're testing everything on the handover checklist. Together."

Mark's fingers moved over the tablet with practiced efficiency, but his body told another story. His shoulders were stiff, held a fraction too high, and his jaw flexed as if bracing against something unseen. His eyes scanned the screen with the kind of focus that wasn't about work; it was more like a daydream or an attempt to hold something at bay.

Zoë had been more than a colleague. The late nights at the hospital and his car parked outside more often than not told their own story. She always called them friends. Mark never said differently.

As we walked the halls for our final checks, the hotel's understated grandeur was impossible to ignore. At eight hundred dollars a night, perfection wasn't a luxury, it was expected. The owners hadn't skimped on the finishes. The rooms boasted marble countertops, gleaming brass fixtures, plush carpet that hushed every step.

When we returned to the conference room, I met each team member's gaze. "Job well done. The client will be happy." I let the words settle before adding, "But more importantly, Zoë would be proud."

For the last two months, I made sure to stop by before Dad worked himself until midnight. Pastor Jonas called it his coping mechanism. He tried getting Dad to talk, but he refused.

Pushing open the door to his office, he glanced up, a small smile lifting the corner of his lips as he pulled off his glasses. "The client's happy with the job. You did well."

"Thanks, Dad." I stepped around the desk and kissed his forehead. "It's almost seven. Let's pop over to the Olive Grove. I'm starving."

His knowing look landed on me. "I see what you're doing. But I'm the one who should be taking care of you."

"Not happening. We take care of each other. Besides, I'll be twenty-seven in two months."

"Old enough to date."

I snorted. "Not interested. Sometimes I wonder if I'm called to singleness. I haven't met a man yet who gives me butterflies or makes my skin tingle."

"Stop reading all those romance novels," Dad scoffed, as he pushed back his chair and stood. "Come on, let's go on one of our famous father-daughter dates." As I hooked my hand through his elbow, he grinned. "Good thing we're heading to my cousin's restaurant. You know how judgy people are; they would assume I'm having a midlife crisis and robbing the cradle."

"Robbing the cradle? You've been spending too much time with Luis and the crew."

He laughed.

"What were you working on?"

The smile vanished. His brows pinched together. "Now that the hotel job is finished, we can take on another. I was talking to the palliative care hospice, seeing if they'd made a decision."

I squeezed his hand. This project meant everything. A way to honor Zoë. Even Mark asked about it. It was the last proposal they worked on together.

"Nothing yet. Rumor has it they might go with another company."

We all wanted that project... but for different reasons.

As we reached the elevator, I pressed the call button. My phone vibrated in my pocket. I pulled it out.

Camila?

My steps faltered. The name hovered in my throat as I stared at the screen.

Dad paused beside me, his brow lifting.

I swiped to answer, flickering somewhere between curiosity and caution. "Hello, Camila." My voice softened, unsure. "I'm stepping into the elevator. Letting you know in case we lose the signal."

She spoke, and I listened, heat prickling the back of my neck as the weight of her words settled in.

Then my stomach knotted. "You want me to do what?"

Dad's eyes searched mine as I scrambled for a response.

My mind screamed, *Say no!* but yes tumbled out.

Why did I say *yes*?

The weight of *yes* settled on me.

Twelve

Bishop

Ten million dollars.

Nathan looked like he might combust from sheer joy. If he weren't in a tux, he'd probably be doing cartwheels.

We stood chatting, champagne swirling in our glasses. The blue cast from the special lighting effects enhanced the virtual reality experience. The moment was surreal.

Camila stepped off the stage after making the shocking announcement.

Sadness. Hurt. Green eyes flashed in front of me.

This would allow us to continue to help other families, ones who wouldn't have to make the same decision Zoë Callos did, hoping to spare her loved ones from grief.

Nathan's hand shot out, gripping mine, his fingers trembling with emotion. "Thank you," he rasped, his voice thick, raw. He swallowed hard, his Adam's apple bobbing. "Thank you.

You've just made me the most popular person with the hospital board. We've raised more than enough to continue the research. And to purchase equipment."

Wesley swaggered toward me, his grin so wide I half-expected his face to split. If his smile got any brighter, I'd need sunglasses in this darkened room.

Raising my glass, I said, "You, Onika, and the team did a fantastic job. Congratulations."

"Thank you. We appreciate the work you've done," Nathan said, extending his free hand to Wesley.

"It's a pleasure to work on something I know will make a real difference," Wesley replied as he clinked his glass.

Guests filtered out to join the dinner crowd, who arrived about thirty minutes ago and were enjoying their predinner cocktails. Before dinner, there would be short stories from women and families the foundation helped in the past year. I always loved hearing those stories, knowing my sister would be proud of the work the foundation continued to do.

I looked forward to what Camila planned for tonight. With two events, we divided to conquer. She handled the dinner while I worked with Wesley and Onika. Camila had been tight-lipped, only dropping little hints. Giving her full control over the dinner was like watching a child in a candy store for the first time.

I stepped onto the garden terrace, cocktails flowing as servers weaved through the crowd holding trays laden with wine and champagne. Mini stations offered hors d'oeuvres, and two bars stood on opposite sides of the garden.

A young lady walked to a microphone set up in the garden. When she opened her mouth, I expected her to sing. Instead, she shared her breast cancer survival story and how the foundation helped support her. At the end, she welcomed everyone and invited them to follow her inside for dinner. A genius move by Camila to have one of our former clients do the welcome.

When I reached our table, where I sat with my parents and some members of the team, Camila slipped into the chair next to mine. As the servers made their way around the room, I leaned over to her and said under my breath, "Nice touch with the welcome."

Before she could respond, our server placed our soups in front of us. As he left, she tilted her head, and a smile turned up the corners of her lips. "Trust me." Batting her lashes at me, she purred, "There is more to come. The night is yet young."

Elena

Dad and the others were at the dinner. Eating before a performance? Never. This wasn't playing with an orchestra ... so why am I so nervous? It was just dinner.

There would be friendly faces in the crowd. Pastor Jonas came with Dad and Imani to offer moral support.

Breathe in ... hold ... out.

I'm talented. God blessed me with this gift. I'm not here as *tokenism*. It's an honor to share my God-given gift.

Then why won't those hateful words leave my head? *Tokenism. She wouldn't be here if not for her mixed background. And being a woman. Checks both boxes. The director believes the orchestra should be a blooming United Nations. Everyone must be represented.* His stuffy, upper-crust accent twisted through my thoughts like a sneer I couldn't shake.

If only I hadn't heard them talking about me. Why did I ever think I'd fit into the orchestra?

Imani and Dad often asked why I turned down the contract to tour with the orchestra. Funny how life works. You can be confident and no-nonsense in one part of your life. Unshakable. And yet, in another, doubt creeps in like it owns the place.

The one person who truly accepted me was gone.

This is for you, Zoë.

I emptied my bladder at least four times in the last three hours. The dinner portion was scheduled for two hours. Two hours of eating. That's a lot of food.

I stood, fingers curling around my flute. Once, it been an extension of me, fluid, effortless. Now, the cool metal pressed against my palm, familiar yet heavy, like it remembered everything I'd tried to forget. I lifted the flute toward my lips.

The door whispered open.

Imani stepped inside, her voice low, steady. "Ready?"

My eyes met hers as something twisted in my stomach, knots tightening with each step toward the door. “Sometimes, I wish I could unhear things.”

She tilted her head, her gaze steady. “Sometimes, those things make you stronger.”

We waited offstage as Camila’s voice boomed through the speakers, delivering the vote of thanks.

“But before we move to the auction, we have one more treat for you.”

Our cue.

Imani walked onto the stage and took her seat at the piano. The first notes of Bach’s *Badinerie* rippled through the air.

I stepped forward, praying the knots in my muscles would unravel. Raising the flute to my lips, my eyes searched for Dad.

But they landed on him.

Alejandro Bishop.

Instead of shifting my gaze, I held his. The knots loosened, one by one, as I lifted the flute ... and the first note hovered in the air.

Thirteen

Elena

"Sold to the lady in red!" the auctioneer pronounced.

The lady beamed. Literally beamed.

Fifty thousand dollars.

She was now the proud owner of an Aimee Patel gown, designed for someone named Topaz Anson. Zoë would certainly know who Aimee Patel was and why the dress was worth that much.

Don't get me wrong, the midnight-blue gown was gorgeous. But fifty thousand dollars?

The dress I wore tonight was expensive by my standards, and it came from Neiman Marcus, on sale, of course. Glancing around the room, the people here were more Merrick Park than Dolphin Mall shopping. So fifty thousand might be a drop in the bucket. But it was all for a good cause.

Up next was a letter opener Imani had been eyeing since we arrived. She planned on leaving here with it.

When bidding jumped to five thousand dollars, she leaned over. "I love it, but that's a little too much to spend on a letter opener, even for me."

The letter opener looked expensive, rich green jade, smooth and polished. Elegant, but eight thousand dollars?

Pastor Jonas barely hesitated. "Ten thousand."

The woman who bid eight thousand shook her head, surrendering.

I tilted my head at Pastor Jonas, who picked up his water glass, unphased by spending ten thousand dollars on a letter opener. He would give it to Imani, I knew that much. She donated her time to help the worship team and refused to be paid.

Pastor Jonas rarely flashed his wealth. His family had very deep pockets, and he owned an expensive vehicle. He picked us up in a Jaguar F-PACE. But on Sundays, he drove a minivan to pick up and drop off church members who didn't have transportation.

He seldom drew attention to himself. But this was for a good cause and was something Imani wanted. And in a room where people were spending fifty grand on a gown, his bid was pocket change.

By the time the auctioneer announced they were at the last item on the list, I had counted over a million raised from the auction alone.

The auctioneer tapped the microphone.

"For those of you who know how we do things here, our final auction item is never in the catalog."

A hush of anticipation fell over the room.

Alejandro Bishop stepped onto the stage. His black tuxedo fit like it was made for him. Sharp lines. Clean cut. Power wrapped in elegance.

The auctioneer's voice carried over the room. "Who wouldn't want a romantic date with an attractive billionaire? Maybe he'll take you out on his yacht."

A woman behind me leaned in and whispered, "I'm bidding for my daughter. She has a crush on him."

Of course, she does.

"Thirty thousand," shouted the lady who claimed she was bidding for her daughter.

These women were ruthless.

"Fifty thousand," came another voice.

Camila.

A voice I knew well by now. She and Bishop were both attractive, worked together, moved in the same circles. It wouldn't be surprising if there was something between them.

The others dropped out of the bid.

Somehow, my gaze locked onto his. It lingered, as if time itself paused, if only for a second. A flicker of something unspoken stirred... fluttered... in me.

No, this couldn't be happening.

Not butterflies.

No, this was the result of an entire day without food. Nothing more.

Hunger. Pure and simple.

Thank you, Jesus, for the clarity.

I repeated the words, willing them to anchor me.

But the truth pressed in anyway. Maybe, just maybe, there was more to this than I wanted to admit.

More than the mere lack of food.

With the auction ending, people stood, some making their way to another room for dancing and more drinks. As Dad rose to leave, a lady bumped into him, and they struck up a conversation. Pastor Jonas and Imani left to claim the jade letter opener.

A good time to slip away.

Rounding the corner, I spotted a short line for the bathroom. I stepped into file behind two women, who were chatting as they waited.

"Thanks for coming with me, Maria. They did so much for my daughter. I had to support," one woman said.

Her friend replied, "I hoped the new treatment would work. But it didn't. What hurts more is how she decided on cremation when it goes against our beliefs. Why didn't she discuss it with me?"

Something nudged at the back of my mind. A strange familiarity. Almost too familiar.

I stepped forward. "Excuse me?"

The woman's eyes widened slightly as she turned to face me. "Oh ... you're the lady that played! It was beautiful. Brought tears to my eyes."

"Thank you. I shouldn't have been listening, and I'm sorry for your loss, but if you don't mind me asking, which hospital was your daughter at?"

Her brows pulled together, probably wondering how this was any of my business.

Fourteen

Elena

Ten.

Fifteen.

The numbers flashed, each one crawling at a snail's pace while my thoughts fired like a hundred race car engines revving at once. The elevator couldn't move fast enough. I called Camila twice when I got into the Uber. But I got no answer. Voicemail both times. Lord, let her be in a meeting.

Camila wouldn't think I was crazy. At least, I hoped not. Maybe she and Alejandro were out to a late lunch.

So what, Elena? That's not important.

This wasn't about Camila or Alejandro. This was about the knot lodged in my gut since the conversation last night, the one that kept tightening, making it hard to breathe no matter what I did to shake it loose.

I tried to forget. I really did. But the tension in my stomach wouldn't ease. It sat there, heavy and tangled, like one giant, coiled ball refusing to budge.

Finally, the elevator *dinged.* The twenty-fifth floor.

I stepped out and tightened my grip on the tablet. I'd made notes. Messy and scattered, but something to start with. We could piece it together, if someone would actually listen. Something was off. I knew it. But trying to make sense of it on my own?

I let out a sigh as I crossed the threshold into the lobby. No ... I needed help.

The day's tension remained with me as I crossed the reception area. The woman behind the desk stood, smoothing her blouse. Her name started with H. Hazel? Maybe Haven? That was what she'd been to me that day.

Steady. Warm. Present.

She glided forward with the grace of someone who had worked high-pressure reception long enough to master the art of kindness without cracks. "Ms. Callos, your performance last night moved me to tears. Camila must have you again next year."

"Thank you." I hesitated, because her name still slipped right through the folds of my mind.

"Helene." Her smile was gentle, not smug. "No need to be embarrassed. When people come here, they're usually under so much pressure. We're often their last hope. You're not the first, or the last, to forget my name."

"Helene," I repeated it with a wince. "Thank you. But I still feel bad."

"If it makes you feel better, I only remembered yours because of the performance. So now we're even." She smiled sheepishly.

I let out a small laugh. "You're great at putting people at ease."

She tilted her head, her eyes soft, and raised one shoulder. "It's part of the job. How can we help today?"

"I'd like to speak with Camila. It's ... important."

Helene's smile dimmed. "Unfortunately, she's on leave for two weeks. Most of the planning team take a break after the gala. A few stay back to tie up loose ends, then they go when the others return." She shook her head, almost apologetically. "Would you like to schedule an appointment?"

I clutched the tablet tighter, heart sinking. "Is there another attorney I can speak with? I just need five minutes. Ten at most."

The air shifted.

A subtle scent drifted through the air, something expensive, masculine, restrained. It was not a cologne that shouted. This whispered. Leather. Vetiver. Maybe cedar. I wasn't sure. I only knew it made the hairs on the back of my neck rise.

Helene's gaze lifted past my shoulder, and that confirmed it.

Someone was behind me.

"Bishop, leaving for the day?" she asked, her tone lighter than a moment ago.

I turned.

He was there.

Alejandro Bishop, in charcoal slacks and a slate-blue dress shirt rolled at the sleeves, stood there like he owned the building, and he probably did.

Our eyes locked.

Dark brown. Not plain. Not soft. Rich, like espresso brewed too strong. The kind that hits you behind the ribs and leaves you buzzing.

Of course, my brain would compare a man to coffee. Dark. Strong. Intense.

Unsettling.

I held my tablet like a shield, not to protect the device, but to stop my hands from trembling. It was official. He made me nervous.

"Ms. Callos."

"Elena," I corrected, holding his gaze and maintaining a firm grip on my tablet.

He nodded slightly. "Ms. Callos, how can we assist?"

Helene interjected quickly. "I was telling her Camila is on leave."

"Thanks, Helene." He glanced toward a family who was near the windows. "Go ahead and assist the family over there. Looks like they've completed their paperwork."

How did he know that? His eyes never left mine.

"So," he said, voice lower now. "How can we help today?"

I glanced at the tablet again. My thumb hovered over the screen like it could offer me confidence. "Last night at the gala ... I overheard something. A woman mentioned her daughter being cremated. It sounded so similar to what happened with Zoë."

His jaw tensed ever so slightly. "Ms. Callos, when I lost my sister, it was hard. We do offer counseling support services—"

"I. Do. Not. Need counseling." I enunciated each word, my eyes narrowing to match his. I held his stare. "Well ... maybe I do. But not for this. Something's wrong. I can feel it."

He studied me. No mocking. No pity. Just observation, like he was trying to work out a puzzle in front of him.

"Or," he said slowly, "it could be coincidence?"

"Never mind." My voice cracked at the edge. I turned in the direction of the elevator.

Chest tight, throat tighter.

I hadn't come here to be judged. Or assessed. Who does he think he is ... a therapist?

"Wait."

I froze mid-step.

His voice softened. Still firm, but not dismissive.

"Let me take a look at what you've got."

I turned around slowly. "Really?"

He nodded toward the tablet. "You brought something, right?"

"Yes. Brief notes."

I expected him to steer me toward a conference room or ask me to email it. Instead, he motioned toward the elevator behind me.

I blinked. "Aren't the offices that way?" I pointed to the hallway he just came from.

A small smirk tugged at his mouth. "I was heading out. Early dinner."

"Oh."

"I assume you can talk and eat at the same time?"

I opened my mouth, then closed it. I didn't know what surprised me more, that he believed me enough to look ... or that he wanted to do it over dinner.

Fifteen

Bishop

Elena's gaze burned the side of my neck from the passenger seat. "Seriously? Going to the Four Seasons? Who does that for a quick meal?"

If she only knew why I was such a frequent patron of the resort.

I stopped the car at the entrance. "Finally, she speaks." I stepped out as an attendant rushed around to assist Elena. Handing over the key fob, I greeted him with a grin. "Hey, Rico. Enjoying married life for me and you?"

He smiled and nodded. "Pulling extra shifts now, with a baby on the way and all."

Rico's gaze flicked to Elena, brows knitting together. I understood the look. I'd never arrived here with a woman before. And certainly not one dressed like her, in black jeans and a matching button-down with CEEL embroidered in bold red thread. Her sister's touch, no doubt.

"Staying long tonight, sir?" Rico asked.

"Not the usual."

Elena tilted her head. "Usual? I'm assuming you're a regular?"

I gestured toward the entrance. "Let's get to the restaurant so we can eat, and you can tell me what you think you've stumbled onto."

I placed my hand on her lower back, and she stiffened. I dropped it. "Sorry. Reflex."

Guiding her through the reception area, I caught the small smirk playing at the corner of her lips, her gaze flicking over the curved floor lamps and sleek lines of the furniture, mentally appraising the lighting design and finding it amusing.

"What?"

"Nothing."

"Don't 'nothing' me. I see that smirk."

She shrugged. "Okay, I admire the minimalist luxury." Smiling, she added, "They have just enough light to keep you relaxed. And enough shadow to make you wonder what the bill will look like."

Leaning closer, I whispered, "The people who come here aren't worried about their card declining."

"True," she chuckled. "There are people like you."

Although she made fun of me, it was the first time I recalled seeing her smile and relax. Something unfamiliar stirred in my chest, a tightness that eased when she smiled, leaving behind an unsettling warmth I couldn't ignore. Even her lips, which were pressed into a firm, no-nonsense line earlier, had softened. Full and expressive, they curved with unexpected ease, pulling something loose in me.

Despite the smile, she was still tightly coiled, like a spring wound to its limit. The rigid, unyielding line of her shoulders bore an invisible weight, and the tension in her jaw was like a vice clamped shut. Her eyes were heavy with unspoken burdens, too heavy for someone her age.

How old was she? Certainly not over thirty. Twenty-five, maybe. Should I look into her family? No. Why waste my time? This was to hear her out so she could go on living her quiet life, doing whatever it was she did.

The restaurant door opened. "Mr. Bishop. Good to see you this evening, sir. Bar?"

"A meeting."

"Follow me. I'll give you a table away from all the action."

"Thank you."

As she leaned in, a faint floral scent lingered, softened and blurred by the weight of a long day. Not unpleasant, just real. The kind of scent that clung to skin after hours of movement and heat, familiar and human in a way that caught me off guard.

"Must be good to be you," she said, a smirk playing on her lips.

When was the last time a woman challenged me? Or annoyed me this much? I liked this volleying between us.

I arched a brow. "Some days. Today doesn't seem to be one of them."

Pulling out the chair for her, I waited as she sat. "Let's order so we can talk while we wait."

I ordered the grand plateau with oysters and crab while she scrunched her nose, studying the menu.

"Trust me, order whatever you want, they'll make it happen."

"Grilled salmon with vegetables and fries."

As the waiter left, I asked, "Who eats grilled salmon with fries?"

She narrowed her eyes. "I do."

Digging into her bag, she pulled out the tablet and scooted her chair next to mine. This section of the restaurant was empty, but even if it weren't, I doubted it would have stopped her.

Pointing at the screen, she said, "Look at the number of cremations in Miami over the last three years." She pulled up a graph with a steady positive slope.

"So, people want a more affordable option," I said.

"Maybe. But there's a common feature in most of these, especially in the last twelve months."

I took the tablet, knowing that if I didn't appear to take this seriously, she would not let this rest. I spent a moment scanning the information, and a faint sense of unease settled in me. There was a clear pattern emerging. Or what Drago would call a profile. Maybe there was something here.

Sixteen

Bishop

A firm knock on the door signaled room service, not Elena. She called fifteen minutes ago when her Uber picked her up. I took the cart from the attendant, tipped him, and closed the door. Her father's business thrived, so why didn't she own a vehicle? Maybe she couldn't drive, though that seemed unlikely. Did she prefer independence, refusing to rely on his money? I'm sure she was paid well as a project manager.

I returned to the table where my laptop sat and reviewed the notes from my conversation with the family from the gala. Hacking into the hotel feed to access the video footage hadn't been difficult. Who would have thought that I would need to use my hacking skills when I was technically on leave from Baas International and working at a not-for-profit supporting cancer patients?

Once I saw who Elena spoke with, I contacted Señor Villarreal. I knew his daughter, Kellie, a devout Catholic four years older than me. Our families attended the same church.

A second knock, firm but tempered, alerted me of Elena's arrival. I opened the door, and she stood there in her signature work attire, her hair pulled into a high ponytail.

Elena was unlike most women I'd been around. She didn't seem to care about impressing anyone with her appearance, certainly not me, especially not in those black safety boots.

She narrowed her eyes. "You really do like the Four Seasons."

I held the door open. "I offered to come to you, but you said no."

"Dad would want to know why you're visiting me."

"And?"

She removed her bag. "I haven't told him about this. I want to keep it between us. If there's something ...I'll let him know."

She set her bag on the side table next to the couch. "I smell food. So, I'm flipping the script this time, let's eat and talk."

"Bossy today, are we?"

"Alejandro."

My name rolled off her lips, sending a shiver down my spine. The softness of it stirred something deep, and I liked the sound of my name on her lips. Shaking my head, I pushed the thought away. Foolishness.

I wheeled the cart toward us and removed the covers. "Salmon with fries, señorita."

She bowed her head for a quick prayer, then picked up a fry and dipped it in ketchup.

"You were about to ask me something?"

She grabbed another fry and raised a brow. "I got strange looks when I said I was here to meet you."

"Oh."

"Don't 'oh' me. I'm not stupid. This is where you hook up with your ladies, right?"

"Used to." I hoped I wasn't that man anymore. After speaking with Roxanne and begging her not to follow my path, I deleted the **GentlemanClub app**.

She kept eating, thankfully dropping the subject.

She placed her fork down, reached for her bag, and pulled out her tablet, leveling her gaze at me. "Don't worry. They took one look at me and knew I wasn't your type."

I smiled. "I have a type?"

"I saw Camila outbid for you."

"Camila and me?" I shook my head. "She's in a committed relationship, ready to walk down the aisle, but definitely not with me."

She arched a brow. "So why bid for you?"

"Story for another time," I said. One she'd never hear, at least not from me. Most people had no idea what went down between Liliana and me. Not even Liliana.

"Anyway. Someone like her. Zoë tried to drill fashion sense into me, but she failed. Don't get me wrong, I know some people find me attractive. But I'm not Zoë or Camila. Forget it ... you wouldn't understand."

She turned on her tablet, casting her eyes toward mine. "Since we spoke last week, I contacted Paula at the hospital. But I want to hear what you found first."

Seventeen

Elena

My stomach lurched, twisting tight, but I forced my face to stay still. Almost. My lips parted slightly, then pressed shut as I clenched my jaw. This sounded like a script for a bad movie.

"Mr. Villarreal said the hospital refused to speak to them. Even the priest."

"Is that even legal?" I asked. "Who refuses to speak with a priest?

Alejandro leaned forward, resting his hands on his thighs. "They're arguing that they're respecting the patient's wishes. But I knew Kellie. Our families attended the same church. She was always a devout Catholic. I can't see her opting to be cremated."

He turned his head, locking eyes with me. "There is no way. The girl never missed Mass. The only reason she probably didn't become a nun or join the Peace Corps or something like that was because of her desire to be a mother. We might be from different social circles, but when it came to church, Father Omar saw us all the same. There were no rich or poor members of his flock."

He smiled. "We all needed confession ... some of us more than others."

I nudged him with my shoulder, smiling to myself. "Why do I feel like you were in the latter group?"

"Me? Never. I was a saint." He chuckled.

I shook my head. Nothing about him screamed "saint." I was certain he was the kind of guy Zoë and I were warned about when we were teenagers. He was TROUBLE.

"What has you smiling?"

"Nothing."

"No, come on. I can tell you're judging me over there." He leaned back on the couch, eyes locked on mine.

I sighed. "Okay, I was thinking that, in your youth, you would have fallen into the category Dad called a 'bad influence,'" I said with air quotes around the two words.

"You wound me."

I rolled my eyes. "Let me tell you what I found."

Alejandro kept his gaze on me as I told him about my visit to the hospital. I arranged for food to be delivered for the nurses.

"Food?"

"We already sent flowers to thank the staff, so I had to do something more. Lunch seemed like a good option."

I filled him in on how it allowed me to speak with Paula, the nurse in charge of the ward. She let it slip that she was surprised by the increase in cremations over the last fifteen months. She blamed the economy.

Leaning back on the couch, I frowned. "What was strange was when Dr. Suleman joined us for lunch. Paula seemed ... scared. Uneasy. We were talking, and all of sudden she tensed up and dropped the subject, even though no one was close enough to hear us."

Alejandro nodded. "Elena, in today's world, you're always in hearing distance of someone. Cameras."

The unease gnawed at me. Deep down, something was off about all these cremations. It couldn't just be the economy. Kel-lie, based on everything Alejandro said, would never have opted for cremation. Neither would Zoë. We had to keep looking into this. Well, I did ... not sure there was a 'we' in this.

I turned my head, resting it against the back of the couch. "What do we do now?"

"Now?" He glanced at his watch. "I take you home."

"Not necessary. I can get a taxi from downstairs."

"Not happening."

I slipped my tablet into my bag, not protesting. Dad would be in bed by now, so I wouldn't have to explain Alejandro's pres-ence. On the drive home, I replayed everything we discussed. There had to be a way to access Kellie's records, something to give her parents proof.

As we approached the gate, I said, "5555."

Alejandro stared at me. I smirked. "I don't think you're a threat. Plus, you're my Watson."

"Why do you get to be Sherlock?"

I laughed.

We pulled into my driveway, parked, and I stepped out. Alejandro surprised me by getting out too, walking me to the door. "You're going all gentleman on me?"

Punching in the code, he said, "Please tell me you use something more secure than 5555."

Before I could respond, my dad crossed the street toward us. He must have been waiting for me to get home. As he stepped into the light, his flushed face came into full view, his eyes shining with urgency. Whatever it was, it mattered more than the fact that a man stood on my doorstep at nearly eleven o'clock. He barely spared Alejandro a glance, offering only a nod of acknowledgment as he followed me inside when I opened the door.

Eighteen

Elena

Alejandro closed the door behind us as Dad reached for my right hand. Dad glowed brighter than a 300-watt bulb, running his other hand through his hair. More silver had threaded through the hair around his temples in the past few months. His grin split wide. "We got it, Elena. We got it!"

Easing my hand out of his grip and embracing Dad, I whispered, "Zoë, you did it. You got it."

I should do a little dance. Or grab my flute and make a joyful noise because this was nothing short of a miracle.

Even in Dad's arms, Alejandro's arm grazed mine, a quiet presence pressing in. Though silent, his energy wrapped around the moment, steady, assessing. When had I become so attuned to him?

Stepping back but still gripping Dad's arms, I asked, "How? I thought they went with another company."

"They did. But that company landed a bigger contract, one that tied up all their resources. So they backed out."

My head tipped back, eyes lifting to the ceiling. "Thank you, Jesus."

Dad nodded. "Before I even knew they'd given the contract to someone else, I sent them an email. Told them how much this project meant to Zoë. It was the last proposal she worked on. Of all of them, this was the one she wanted most because of her own illness." He shook his head, something reverent in his voice. "Who says the personal touch doesn't work?"

Alejandro finally spoke, voice low, controlled. "Congrats, Theo. I can see why this calls for a celebration tonight."

Dad exhaled, his expression sobering. "Yes and no." His gaze shifted back to me. "No, because you're not going to like the next part." He gave me that tight, sideways smile, the kind he wore when delivering news I wouldn't like. "The project planning meeting is coming up, and they want us there."

I expected that. Mark, Sophie, and I needed to attend. These meetings usually came with at least a month's notice, which meant it wouldn't be until June.

Alejandro shifted, barely a movement but enough to register.

My gaze flicked to him. By then, we'd have made progress with our investigation. Either there was something more to the increase in cremations, or there wasn't. I hoped there wasn't. But my gut told me otherwise.

I dropped my hands from Dad's arms and walked further into the living room. "When is the meeting? I'll brief Mark and

Sophie tomorrow. We'll go over the proposal and fine-tune any details before June. Did they send any additional information?"

Dad shook his head. "No. The meeting is Thursday."

A slow pulse of unease coiled through me. No wonder he gave me a tentative smile. My eyes snapped to him. "As in... the day after tomorrow? Thursday? That would mean leaving tomorrow evening."

He hesitated. "Also..." His voice hitched. "It's not at their corporate office. They're holding it in Pensacola, where they're building the facility."

Dad kept talking, but his voice blurred into white noise.

The project was important. But the hospitals, the investigation...Zoë.

This would stall everything.

Paula agreed to lunch, a chance to talk away from the hospital. She'd been willing to talk the day I brought lunch for them, until Dr. Suleman showed up. She shut down like a television losing its signal.

Alejandro's eyes stayed on me.

I turned to Dad."Organizing all that and working on the proposal in two days?"

Sinking into the couch. I had to do this project. I had to keep searching. For Zoë. For all the other families. The room tightened around me, the air thick with unspoken tension. My chest rose and fell, too fast, too shallow. Every second stretched, straining under pressure I couldn't name, like something inside me was bracing to break.

Alejandro's voice was quiet but firm. "I might have a solution. I own a property in Pensacola. You can stay there. I haven't been down there in a while."

My eyes snapped to his.

He didn't look away. His gaze held mine, steady, measured, unreadable.

Nineteen

Bishop

Elena. Her high ponytail swayed slightly as she leaned in, the curve of her neck graceful as she spoke to Mark.

He sat too close. Shift any closer and he would practically be in her lap. Okay, not in her lap. They sat opposite each other, a table between them, documents spread out.

Still too close.

And her mouth, serious and focused and slightly parted as she spoke, wasn't helping. The way her lips moved, deliberate and precise, stirred something low in my chest. I shouldn't be noticing details like that.

Shaking my head, I tore my gaze away and forced myself to focus on the clouds outside the window. Why did it matter? How had this escalated from her staying at my house ... to using my plane ... to me tagging along? There was no real reason for me to be here. I could've arranged for the house to be ready for them.

Yet here I was, thirty minutes from landing in Pensacola.

Somehow, when Elena mentioned that Sophie could no longer travel due to a client emergency, the idea popped into my head to come along. Mark might be a nice guy ... but this was my idea.

Better for me to be here.

The setting might make him all romantic. One thing could lead to another. The house was set away from everyone else. And Elena would be there alone.

Well, not alone. Alone with him.

Great. Now I sounded like a jealous boyfriend. I shook my head. No, this wasn't jealousy. It was *concern*. I wanted her to feel safe. It was definitely better for me to be here.

Elena's voice pulled me back. "They'll ask if we can shave anything off the project."

Mark shook his head.

"We need to be firm," she said. "Cutting costs will compromise the project... safety. This is a healthcare facility. They need a solid electrical plan."

While they attended their meetings, I could relax. In the evenings, I could take them out to dinner. Maybe even do some work on the project Elena and I started.

In my field, I don't jump to conclusions. I need facts. We have suspicious information but nothing concrete yet. But knowing the Villarreal family, Kellie opting for cremation was as likely as humans living on Pluto.

The captain announced our descent, and Elena and Mark packed up. She leaned back and closed her eyes, her lips moving silently, probably praying for a safe landing. Her brow furrowed, her lashes fanned above her cheeks. I watched the subtle movement of her lips, drawn to the quiet rhythm. Something about the way she folded into stillness made the cabin noise fade for a moment, like she was in a different world entirely, and I was intruding just by noticing.

By the time we reached the house, the sky had deepened to navy, and the air was thick with the scent of salt and distant sea spray. Elena stepped onto the terrace, her gaze sweeping over the endless expanse of water.

"Wow," she murmured, tucking a strand of hair behind her ear.

Mark let out a low whistle. "This is the life."

I led them inside, showing them their rooms and mentioning that dinner would be on the patio in an hour, giving us time to settle in and change.

After showering and putting on a pair of jeans and a T-shirt, I entered the kitchen. I slid the seafood pasta bake the housekeeper left in the fridge into the oven and took out a few things to make a green salad.

Elena walked in wearing white jeans and a gray long-sleeved V-neck shirt. It wasn't low-cut, but somehow the fabric clung in all the right places. She moved like she didn't even realize it, completely unaware of the small havoc she caused just by walking into a room.

Focus, Bishop ... before you lose a finger, of all things, making a salad.

She stepped into the kitchen. "Let me do something. You're not here to play host and feed us."

I pointed to the cutlery. "You can set the table."

When she passed behind me, we didn't touch. But having her that near made me pause my chopping and take a deep breath. Ten minutes later, Elena and I brought the items out for dinner.

Mark swirled his wine before taking a slow sip then set the glass back on the table with a satisfied sigh. "Bishop. Man, if I were you, I'd be down here every weekend." He turned to Elena. "Boss, with a house like this, I would work remotely and only come in when necessary."

"Dad is the boss."

His ease with Elena grated on me. He seemed like a decent guy, but their closeness – that I didn't like.

I forced a chuckle, keeping my expression neutral. He had no idea how close he was to getting on my nerves. The way he leaned in, too familiar, too comfortable with her.

I nodded. "It is beautiful. Maybe I should spend more time here."

We dined on the patio off the infinity pool where potted jasmine vines curled up the columns, their sweet scent mixing with the salty breeze. The Gulf of Mexico stretched endlessly beyond us, moonlight rippling across the waves. The rhythmic crash of the surf below set a steady pulse to the evening.

Elena set her fork down. "Thank you for everything. My room could rival any five-star hotel."

"Glad you like it."

I placed them at opposite sides of the house, with my room next to Elena's. Like I was protecting her virtue.

Protecting it from whom? Mark?

This wasn't the 1800s. Who was I fooling?

Twenty

Elena

My internal alarm went off like clockwork. I reached for my phone. Yep, a few minutes before 5:30 a.m. Swinging my feet to the floor, a smile tugged at my lips. Coffee, prayer, and my Bible: my sacred morning ritual. The only difference? Instead of curling up on my living room sofa, this morning I will get to do it while watching the sun rise over the Gulf of Mexico.

I pulled on soft yoga pants and a matching long-sleeved tee, grabbed my tablet, and padded downstairs.

The rich, velvety scent of coffee curled through the air, wrapping around me before I even reached the kitchen. Not any coffee, but the good stuff. Bold, dark, with hints of toasted caramel and something deep and earthy. The kind that promised warmth before the first sip even touched my lips.

The house's welcoming silence greeted me. Alejandro must have set it on a timer before going to bed. Moving toward the kitchen, as much as the aroma of the coffee pulled me, I couldn't help but admire the copper pendant lights suspended above the island, their hammered surfaces catching and throwing back golden flecks of dawn. Below them, the island stretched out, a single slab of creamy marble veined with bronze, its base a muted seafoam green. This house, with all its open space and beautiful views, was an interior designer's dream.

Inhaling the coffee as I poured, I murmured, "God, I'm not coveting, but I need to take some of this stuff home with me. On my budget, whatever this is, I for sure can't afford it." Picking up an insulated mug to keep my coffee as warm as long as possible, I moved toward the patio.

A salty breeze wrapped around me, carrying the gentle hush of waves rolling onto the shore. The world remained untouched, hushed, as if creation itself held its breath in reverence. The water rippled in shifting hues of deep indigo, soft lavender, and gold as the first light of dawn broke over the horizon. I wished I could paint. Words couldn't capture this.

Studying this masterpiece, there could be no doubt there was a God who created all of this. Closing my eyes, the coffee and the salty air brought a calmness that had been absent for months. I hadn't even realized it was missing until this moment.

Movement.

Noise. Faint to the ear. It pulled my eyes to the source.

Gliding through the infinity pool, Alejandro moved toward me, pausing when he saw me. Then, he swam closer.

"Up early," he commented.

My throat forgot how to form words. I nodded. The hint of morning light played across his golden skin, making it look almost mythical.

His brows pulled together as he hoisted himself out of the pool. My eyes pulled to him like an iron to a magnet. Droplets traced the cut of his chest, sliding toward the deep V of his abs. I looked away. Can I even erase this memory? Something pulled at the edge of my thoughts... Do you really want to?

Yes.

No.

"Everything okay?"

No. The word screamed in my mind. One moment, I could be thinking about God's creation, and the next ... the next what? I didn't even know. Dad and Zoë always questioned why I never dated. Their curiosity laced with a concern I never knew how to explain.

It was complicated.

Being given up for adoption as a result of a teenage pregnancy. My faith. Never being attracted to a man. I thought maybe I was called to singleness.

Growing up, our parents took us to the beach. I had seen other men without a shirt. But no one had ever made my throat dry or my pulse stutter. My fingers tightened around the mug as if it could anchor me. I forced a sip; the warmth traveling through me, but it did nothing to steady the trembling awareness creeping under my skin. Heat rose to my face, betraying the sudden, unfamiliar shift inside me.

Twenty-One

Bishop

My gaze caught on the Vince Flynn novel I finished yesterday, the first book I'd read in maybe two years. A forgotten habit. I had ordered the last five books in the series, but this was the first one I cracked open.

Yesterday, for the first time in years, I stopped. Just for me. No work. No obligations. Silence. And surprisingly, it was good. I even woke early for a swim, slicing through the cool morning water until Elena stepped onto the patio. She didn't say a word. The moment I climbed out, she turned and disappeared inside.

When she and Mark returned from their meeting, he and I sat in the kitchen, drinking Coronas. But Elena never showed up for dinner.

This morning, there were no early appearances, no fleeting glances or hesitant exchanges. Just her in the kitchen, making breakfast. She stood at the counter, chopping something and humming a tune I didn't recognize. Knife in hand, she chopped steadily, shoulders relaxed, her body swaying slightly in rhythm. Whatever weighed her down yesterday had lifted.

She glanced up, and my chest clenched.

A small smile. A gesture to the pan in front of her. "I'm making breakfast for us. Nothing fancy. Sautéed potatoes with sausage."

Given her skittish behavior yesterday morning, I went out to the patio to give her some space. After breakfast, I dropped Mark and Elena off at the hotel and took the long way back. I wasn't ready to return to the empty beach house. Drago would laugh and say I was getting sappy in my old age.

Eventually, I pulled the vehicle into the driveway and sat for a moment appreciating the waves.

Sappy ... Yup!

Walking into the kitchen, I grabbed my laptop from the island. Sitting on the L-shape sofa, I nudged the book I was reading aside. Yesterday had been a rare indulgence, but another day of idleness? Not happening. Elena was deep into the work project. At least I could comb through the data we gathered on the cremations, reminding her this investigation wasn't forgotten.

It kept my hands busy, my mind focused, and boredom at bay. I never understood how people managed week-long vacations. I never leased this place out for long-term rentals in case I wanted to pop over. I rarely did. But with the clear waters stretching out in front of me, it was the perfect vacation home.

Villarreal family. It would give them peace, hopefully. And putting all this to rest might actually give Elena true closure.

Camila returned next week. I considered asking her to work on behalf of the Villarreal family to get the documents. The legal route would take weeks. Why wait when I could ...

I flicked my gaze to the corner of my screen. A challenge. How long would it take to slip into Southshore Memorial Hospital's records undetected?

Forty-five minutes. That was all it took.

Their system had modern two-factor authentication, but no AI monitoring. I expected more.

Too easy.

I downloaded Kellie's records. Another file labeled *Cremations* caught my eye. I downloaded that too, then opened it.

A list of names.

A shiver trickled down my spine. My arms tensed, skin prickled. Some names bore an *X*. Others, a checkmark.

What did the *X* mean?

I scanned down the list until I got to: Kellie Villarreal, *X*.

My eyes darted across the screen, scanning names, birthdates. Clicking on the *X* brought up a report. All the names with an *X* appeared there. Strangely, the cancer diagnoses were missing for these ones. Instead, in its place were two letters.

The same two letters, for all of them.

Twenty-Two

Elena

The project director droned on, rehashing points we covered an hour ago, his voice a monotonous hum of statistics and projections. My fingers curled into my lap, itching to check my phone again to see if Alejandro had an update. Two hours had crawled by since a message lit up my screen, telling me he found something strange. I wanted to shout for joy when the project director finished his presentation, signaling the end of the meeting.

Yesterday morning by the pool, I bolted like some foolish adolescent, like I'd never seen a shirtless man before.

Seeing a man without a shirt wasn't the same as seeing Alejandro without one. Water streamed down his sculpted frame, each drop tracing the ridges of muscle like it had a destination. I shut my eyes, trying to blot out the image. Don't think about him. Don't think about the pool. The water. The way it beaded on his skin like diamonds. I popped my eyes open. Clearly, that didn't work. If anything, it sharpened the image. I could almost smell the chlorine still clinging to him. Why did God have to make him so fine? Unfair.

The client offered to take the entire team to the Pensacola Beach boardwalk. Mark had been eager for the change of scenery, but I, on the other hand, could only think about Alejandro. Well, Alejandro and the message. Even if he hadn't found something, I would've gotten a ride back to the beach house anyway. Let them drink the night away.

Leaving the conference room, they went in one direction, and I got into the vehicle they arranged to take me back to the beach house. Last night, I avoided him. But after praying and giving myself a stern talking-to, I admitted that of all the men I've worked closely with over the years, for some strange reason, he unsettled me the most. And in my line of work, I met a lot of men.

Take this trip, for example. Aside from the client's two executive assistants, I was the only woman at the table. Years of navigating spaces dominated by men had solidified my confidence. Yet, there was something about Alejandro that pulled me in different directions, as if I were going through puberty again instead of turning twenty-seven in a few months.

After all, there was a reason the man had a hotel room he rented long-term for his hookups.

I closed my eyes again and took a deep breath, trying to untangle the chaotic thoughts swirling in my mind. As the tension began to melt away, a gentle wave of tranquility washed over me. I turned my attention out the car window, watching the scenery blur past. The late afternoon sun cast long shadows over the road. Palm trees lined the streets, their fronds swaying in the warm breeze. A group of tourists strolled along the sidewalk, their sunburned faces glowing as they laughed over something that probably wouldn't be funny once the margaritas wore off.

I sighed and forced my gaze back to the road, but my thoughts strayed again to Alejandro and the message, each possibility spinning through my mind. As the beach house came into view, I grabbed my messenger bag and slung it across my body. After tipping the driver, I stepped out and rushed inside.

"Alejandro," I whisper-shouted, stepping farther into the house. A rich, savory aroma curled through the air, a blend of garlic, butter, and toasted parmesan, making my stomach stirred in anticipation. The scent lured me toward the kitchen. Whatever he was cooking made my taste buds water.

Reaching the kitchen, I caught him pulling a crusted piece of meat from a pan. A smile tugged at my lips. "Alejandro Bishop, is that Parmesan-crusted chicken? *You* can cook?"

Turning off the stove, he lifted his eyes to mine. "Not only can I cook," he said, his gaze steady and a hint of challenge in his voice, "I can do it well."

Is there anything he couldn't do well? My brain went back to his hotel room. I cleared my throat. "Need any help?"

"Dinner will be ready in ten. Go change. We'll eat and talk."

I rested a hand on my hip. "You know, talking with you always seems to involve food."

His dark eyes settled on me. "Do you object? Maybe I enjoy feeding you."

Heat crept up my neck, and I darted from the room. After a quick shower, I slipped into a long summer dress with thin straps and returned, ready for both food and whatever he discovered today.

As I reentered the room, he was plating the food, like he was on some cooking show that judged on presentation. He really took his cooking seriously.

"At least it looks good ... Michelin Star worthy," I teased.

He positioned his laptop on the island between our place settings.

Settling onto the tall chair, I offered a quick prayer to bless the food, then I took a bite. A soft sound escaped before I could stop it. "My gosh. You can cook. The scents were heavenly, but I wasn't sure that translated into good-tasting food."

Throwing back his head, he laughed. The rich sound rolled through the space, smooth and unguarded. A faint shiver traced down my spine. I gave myself a small shake, as if I could dislodge the feeling. Whatever strange effect he had on me, I wasn't ready to examine it.

After a few more bites, no matter how good the food tasted, I needed to know what he found.

As if reading my mind, he reached for his laptop, scanned his finger, and information filled the screen. He pointed. "Tell me what you see."

I ran my eyes over the data. A question formed, how had he gotten this? But as I studied the screen, that thought vanished.

Twelve.

All women.

Their ages ranged from twenty-five to thirty-seven.

The last column made the food curdle in my stomach. Lifting my eyes to Alejandro, I whispered, "All these women were cremated?" In the last column, which listed the diagnosis, the same two letters appeared for each woman. "PC," I said aloud. I stared at him as a wave of nausea threatened. "Does that mean what I think it means?"

"What are you thinking?" His fingers grazed mine, tentative, like he wasn't sure he should touch me at all. His eyes searched my face, lingering too long, as if bracing for something he didn't want to hear or believing I held the answer. Maybe it was me who didn't want to hear what was already running through my mind.

"PC... Pancreatic cancer..."

Twenty-Three

Bishop

Elena jolted upright, the chair scraping against the floor with a sharp screech. She clamped a hand over her mouth. Her eyes widened in panic before she rushed from the kitchen, her footsteps pounding against the hardwood. A sharp instinct kicked in, my body moving before my brain could catch up. I wasn't used to feeling helpless, and I didn't like it. The harsh sound of her retching and muffled sobbing pulled me toward the first guest bathroom. She hunched over the toilet, her shoulders shaking, as tears trailed down her cheeks.

I crouched beside her, sweeping her hair back and securing it with the band holding her ponytail. It was a simple, automatic motion, something to do while I ignored the tightness in my chest. My arms circled her as she sagged against me, drained.

"Shh ..." Rubbing her back gently, I whispered, "Finished?"

She nodded. I flushed the toilet and let her sit while I took out a toothbrush and toothpaste for her. I helped her up. She brushed her teeth and washed her face. I handed her a towel. Her eyes met mine in the mirror, and I asked, "Ready?" It made no sense to ask if she was okay; it was obvious she wasn't. I wasn't in the habit of asking stupid questions.

Wrapping an arm around her as she leaned into me, I walked her to the guest room. The ocean air filled the space, drifting in from the open balcony doors. "Let's sit out on the patio."

Settling onto the daybed, I pulled her toward me. Elena rested her head on my chest, as if she found comfort in human touch... my touch. The last person I'd held this close was my sister. Not even when Liliana and I dated. The dating and relationship were real for me. Unfortunately for Liliana, it was just for show. That was probably why we never experienced this kind of closeness. It had all been fake.

Although the circumstances were different from my sister's, Elena carried the same quiet trust, the same unspoken need for comfort. Just like then, the weight of someone leaning on me settled deep. Her grief pressed into my chest, as if I could absorb it, take some of it away. The night air clung to my skin. The scent of salt thickened in my lungs. Elena curled into me, her body fitting perfectly against mine. I kissed her forehead, slow and soft.

Seconds ... minutes slipped by as we stayed there. When she shivered, I reached for a blanket resting on the arm of the chair and pulled it over her. She snuggled into me.

The rhythmic crash of waves against the shore blended with the chirping of crickets and the distant rustling of palm leaves, framing the moment in a steady rhythm.

"Zoë's mum died from pancreatic cancer. Lived only a few weeks after her diagnosis. They found it late. So, Zoë was screened every year from the time she was twenty. That allowed for early detection."

She snuggled deeper into me, her hand brushing against my chest. I took a slow breath.

"We thought we beat it." Her voice softened. "Then it came back last year. After seven years, it returned with a vengeance."

Pancreatic cancer. *PC.* Her reaction. It clicked.

Nathan sent the documents showing authorization for the cremation. But at the time we didn't check for her sister's diagnosis.

If Elena's right, this might be bigger than we thought.

She sat up, and instantly, I missed the weight of her head on my chest.

Seriously, what was wrong with me?

I could stop pretending, at least to myself. If to no one else, I could admit it to myself.

I'm attracted to her. Elena.

Her eyes lifted to mine. "Something's going on at that hospital."

"This hospital has nothing to do with Zoë."

"Maybe Zoë's case was legitimate. But something is off."

One thing was for sure, Elena Callos had no plans of letting this go, and honestly, I could not blame her.

We'd stumbled into something, that much I was certain about.

Twenty-Four

Elena

"¡Hola! You've reached Paula. I'm probably working or ignoring my phone. Leave a message or shoot me a text. I'll get back to you. ¡Gracias!"

Monday evening I settled into the soft leather seat and buckled my seatbelt, the events of the past two days replaying in my mind. Friday night stretched far behind me, but its weight clung to me even now, settling deeper as the plane made its final checks before takeoff. I had talked to God, but unease coiled tight in my chest, refusing to loosen. The file. Somehow, Alejandro had gotten his hands on it. I didn't know how, but maybe it was best left that way.

And then there was me, wrapped in his embrace. There's no use lying to myself. I loved how safe his arms and chest made me feel. And finally, the growing attraction between us. I had never been in a relationship, but I wasn't naive.

Alejandro and I agreed to speak with Paula, the nurse in charge at the hospital where my sister was. Saturday afternoon, I had called and left a message. She had been with a patient. I followed up with a text, inviting her to lunch on Tuesday. I planned to leave here Monday, even if the work wasn't finished. Mark agreed to stay and handle any final details.

I pressed the phone off and switched it to airplane mode. "You think I should stop by the hospital tomorrow?"

Alejandro raised a brow. "Why?"

"She hasn't returned my call. Doesn't strike me as the type to ignore a message. Not very professional."

The hostess approached, inquiring if we wanted anything before takeoff. I ordered a Coke with lemon; Alejandro, a glass of wine.

"Can I suggest closing your eyes and not worrying for this flight? You worked all day, and we came straight here."

"I'm not worried about the project. Mark will stay until Wednesday."

"Sunday."

"Sunday?" I echoed. He must have really loved it there.

"He asked if he could stay and finish out the week."

"Smart move. If meeting Paula wasn't so pressing, I wouldn't want to leave." I reached over and touched his hand. "It's a beautiful home. You should visit more often."

Before I could pull back, his fingers closed around mine, a quiet hold that sent a ripple of warmth through me. My pulse skipped, just a fraction, before settling into a steady rhythm, hyperaware of his touch. Did he realize he still held my hand? The hostess returned with our drinks, breaking the moment. Taking his advice, I closed my eyes, letting the hum of the plane lull me to sleep.

A few minutes from landing, a soft caress traced over my hand. My left hand still rested in his.

"You were frowning in your sleep."

"Don't tell me I was talking."

"Rambling about how you'll take over and save the world."

I pulled my hand back, the warmth vanishing too quickly. Before I could dwell on it, I playfully punched his shoulder, masking the sudden emptiness with a smirk.

We picked up food to bring back home after leaving the airport because I knew there was none in my fridge. Opening the front door, I spotted fresh flowers resting on the table and a note on the newspapers.

"Looks like someone has an admirer."

Trying to take my suitcase from him, I teased, "Jealous?"

The corners of his mouth lifted. "I'll put this upstairs for you."

Before I could insist it wasn't necessary, he was already moving up the stairs. I paused in the hallway, a crease forming between my brows. Dad's vehicle wasn't in the driveway. He always wanted an update at the end of each day. Something must have kept him at the office, or he would be camped out at my door.

Alejandro descended the stairs. "Let's eat and figure out a strategy now that you've had some rest. And we have food."

"I remember. Talking and eating."

The rich aroma of golden, crispy spring rolls and the savory scent of sautéed shrimp with garlic and vegetables curled into the air, teasing my senses. My stomach stirred like a waking beast in response, the warm spices promising comfort after a long day.

I glanced at the clock, just shy of nine. "Maybe I should try calling her again."

Dialed. No answer. Showing up at the hospital unannounced carried too much risk, but if I could get her alone, she'd be more willing to talk.

Alejandro carried the garbage to the kitchen. More than likely, the flowers were from Imani. Even though Dad lived next door, she often checked on the house when I was away. Reading the note, I smiled. *Missed you. Hope you had a good time. Love, Imani.*

"Who still gets print papers?"

"We do. Dad has a subscription, and we all read the same paper. Family tradition."

"I'm only reading Monday's." I tossed the others into the recycling bin.

We settled into the living room, the rustle of the newspaper breaking the silence as Alejandro leaned forward. "Tomorrow, I'm going to track down some of the families from the list, see if they have a similar story. You focus on Paula."

Alejandro's eyes dropped to the paper. A crease formed between his brows. Following his gaze, I caught the headline at the top of the front page: *Speculation Mounts: Will Jameson Wakefield Announce His Senate Run?* The caption hovered over a picture of a stately couple. The man exuded power, his sharp suit tailored to perfection, his expression a practiced mask of confidence. The woman at his side wore a dress that clung to her like armor. Her smile was tight, never reaching the distant gaze in her eyes. She stood poised, polished and trapped, as though she longed to escape but knew there was no way out.

Shaking his head, Alejandro muttered, "Slime. Pure slime. He won't be elected. Over my living body."

"Guess you two have history?"

"Actually, I can say I've never met the man. Maybe that's why he thinks his run for the Senate is possible."

To ease the tension, I flipped the paper. My gaze landed on the back page. Air stalled in my throat, a sharp hitch, as the headline seared into my vision.

Nurse killed in mugging.

What?

A chill rippled down my spine, tightening my chest like a vice. My fingers clenched around the paper. Goosebumps dotted my skin. The words blurred, swallowed by the pounding in my ears. Alejandro eased it from my grip, his voice distant as he read.

"Paula Herrera, a nurse at St. Andrews Hospital, was attacked after working overtime to save someone's life ...only to have her own taken in a mugging gone wrong ..."

Twenty-Five

Bishop

Elena's breath snagged. Her fingers dug into my wrist, her grip tight, then suddenly weak.

"No. No. This can't be."

The words barely escaped, but the anguish behind them was deafening. The newspaper slipped from my hand, drifting to the floor.

Elena didn't move. Her body locked up, shoulders drawn tight, hands twitching slightly, as if unsure whether to grasp something or let go. Her breath came in quick, uneven bursts, a sharp contrast to the eerie stillness of the room.

I pulled her onto my lap, her frame stiff at first, then gradually slackening as the shock settled in.

"She was always kind to us," Elena said, her voice low. "The first person Zoë connected with on that floor."

A shudder ran through her, fine tremors rippling beneath my fingertips. I pressed a kiss to her forehead, cool dampness meeting my lips.

"I don't understand why people steal," she whispered into my chest. "But if they have to ... why not just take the things and go? She didn't deserve that."

Her shaking slowed, and her breathing evened out. Elena might believe this was a random act. But until I spoke with the CEO tomorrow, I wasn't ruling anything out. Jaden, Drago, or I could stage a hit and make it look like a mugging. It all depended on the message we wanted to send. In our world, nothing happened by chance.

She sniffled and lifted her gaze, eyes glistening with unshed tears. "The weight of the day... Paula's senseless death... they've drained my last ounce of energy. A headache is creeping in." She rubbed her temples. "I should sleep. Or at least try to."

"Close your eyes."

"Don't you have to go home? Plus, you must be uncomfortable with me on your lap."

Kissing her head again, I whispered, "Close your eyes."

If she thought I'd leave her in this house alone, without knowing what happened at that hospital or understanding the security here, she was dead wrong. No chance.

A few minutes later, her breathing slowed, soft and steady. Her body shifted, limbs gone slack with the kind of heaviness we call dead weight. I eased her onto the couch, then went upstairs, grabbed a spread and pillow, and tucked her in.

I sank onto the rug beside her, exhaling deeply. Plush carpet. A roof overhead. The steady hum of the AC.

I shifted, adjusting to the rug beneath me, the firmness grounding. This was luxury. Drago and I slept in worse. Mud up to our elbows in a foxhole, ribs grinding against frozen earth. Jungle floors crawling with fire ants. Collapsed buildings that smelled of death, concrete cold against our backs. Cargo containers reeking of rust and old fuel.

This? This was five-star living ...

I woke up to a faint vibration. Then an alarm blaring. I shot up, rushed to the island, and silenced her phone before it could disturb her. At least we both got some much-needed rest.

Picking up her phone, the screen flashed 5:30 a.m. Why in heaven's name was her alarm set for that time?

At least I got up that early to work out. God knows what she did at this hour. I pulled out my phone and texted to see if my sparring partner and trainer could come around 9:00 a.m. This week, I needed to focus on finding out more about what we'd stumbled into.

Rustling came from where Elena lay. "I slept."

A small smile tugged at my lips. "Yes, you certainly did. I'm your Sleep Number bed set at 55. Not too hard or soft. Just right. Perfect for falling sleep on."

She rolled her eyes and jerked upright. "Thank you. For staying." Stretching, she asked, "Where did you sleep?"

Placing her feet on the rug, she stood. I smirked. "Why are you trampling my bed?"

"You're crazy. You slept on the floor?"

"I'm going to get my suitcase. Can I use your bathroom?"

She nodded. "Dad will probably be over. I'm sure he saw your car when he got home."

Being around Elena centered me, like an anchor pulling me from chaos. With her, the world slowed, sharpened, became something worth protecting. She brought out a protective side of me, the kind only reserved for those I deeply cared about. The people I'd stand in front of a machine gun and take every bullet for.

As I shut my car trunk, Theo stepped outside. I drove the Mercedes SUV. Needed the space for the luggage.

"Everything okay?" he asked.

He met my extended hand with a firm shake. "Not really," I replied. "Elena got some news last night that shook her."

"What news?"

"The nurse that was killed. Yesterday's newspaper."

"Sorry. Imani took over all the papers. I didn't get to read Monday's. I left early for a project issue."

"It was one of the nurses who worked on your daughter's floor. Paula."

His face paled. "Paula?"

He turned and hurried inside. "Elena. I just heard." He wrapped his daughter in a hug.

Leaving them, I made my way to the guest bathroom I spotted last night. A marble vanity speckled with green and browns, and a shower with a rainforest showerhead. A fully stocked cabinet with extra toiletries and toothpaste.

I rolled my shoulders, the tension from the past twenty-four hours refusing to loosen. Stripping, I stepped into the shower, letting the hot water pound against my neck and back, willing it to wash away the weight of everything unraveling around us. My first call after my trainer would be to Nathan. For now, I needed to focus on getting information about Paula. I had known Nathan for nearly two decades. I would hate to think, if anything was going on, he was involved. But I've learned over the years that money and power would make a saint sell his soul and sleep soundly after.

Twenty-Six

Elena

When Alejandro came downstairs, he drank only coffee, skipping breakfast before his training session. From all the time I'd spent against his chest recently, I couldn't deny the muscles packed beneath his shirt.

Dad suggested I stay home, but the idea of being alone unsettled me. Paula's senseless death already wreaked havoc on my mind. I needed to keep occupied. Mark sent updates as agreed. The project director wanted to know if I would rejoin them. If needed, I could easily videoconference into the meeting.

The air shifted, a barely-there difference. I paused, glancing up. Then Dad entered, carrying a crate with two cups of coffee and a bag I would bet a hundred dollars contained a coconut and raisin scone.

Settling into the chair opposite me, he said, "Ellie, you should have stayed home. This project is important, but so are you to me."

I took the coffee as he opened the bag. I didn't want to worry him, but today, I needed to be around people. Which was unlike me. I could have stayed home, played my flute, read, or caught up on the YouTube channels I followed, all nestled in the Bible Nerd corner of the internet. Leading a Sunday School class for older teens aged fifteen to seventeen, I followed discussions on apologetics. I even completed a diploma in Bible studies. Those young ladies kept me on my toes with their questions.

Dad sipped his coffee, eyes steady on me. "Do you like him?"

I could pretend I didn't know who he meant, but Dad knew I was sharp, a trait I inherited from my biological mother. No sense playing dumb now.

Breaking off a piece of the scone, I rolled it between my fingers, stalling. The buttery crumbs pressed into my fingertips as I finally popped it into my mouth, chewing slowly, hoping it would buy me enough time to steady my thoughts. I expected this conversation, surprised it hadn't come up earlier. Finding Alejandro's vehicle still in my driveway this morning meant I couldn't put it off any longer.

"He's not a Christian."

Dad sipped his coffee before resting it on the desk. "When Zosia and I went on our first date, I could've been Satan's personal imp," Dad chuckled. "Our fathers set it up. She was so different from me. I wanted to party... she wanted to pray. I'm certain that back then, praying for my soul topped her list." He shook his head. "Guess it worked."

I got up and sat next to him. "I could have sworn God called me to singleness. For the first time in my life, I'm questioning it."

I admired Imani's unwavering strength, how she turned her deepest regret into a calling, pouring love into every young woman who crossed her path. And Pastor Jonas' wisdom wasn't only in his sermons but in the way he lived, his quiet acts of kindness shaping lives in ways no one ever noticed until they needed it most.

Imani committed her life to the church after getting pregnant and giving me up for adoption. When I finally agreed to meet her at eighteen, I didn't want to like her. But I couldn't help it. From that day on, she became a constant in my life, stepping in and helping our family, especially when my adoptive mom got sick.

I've admired both of them. Their walk. A walk of singleness, as if their only calling was to serve God and others. I wanted to be so much like them.

Dad patted my thigh. "Maybe God is showing you a different path."

The words settled between us, quiet but heavy. I stared at the coffee cradled in my hands.

A different path.

Twenty-Seven

Bishop

Camila strolled into my office, grinning like a five-year-old who had eaten a handful of gummy bears. "How was your trip?" she asked.

If I hadn't burned off the restless energy sparring, I might've told her to take her bubbly, teasing self elsewhere. Instead, I took the files from her and ignored her. There was nothing to share with anyone until Elena and I had a heart-to-heart conversation. I needed to know where we stood. I was certain this could not all be one-sided.

We hadn't discussed strategy last night, but I called Nathan today. His hands were full with family, staff, and clients; everyone wanted to know if they were safe. He mentioned a mugging two years ago but assured me they had guards patrolling and cameras everywhere.

Cameras.

I spent the afternoon hacking into his system, pulling footage from twelve hours before and after the incident. It would take some time, but I would sieve through the surveillance video tomorrow. The footage would let me know if this was random, or if we were dealing with a professional.

I dropped a work file on the kitchen island. I'd take it to the home office later. I washed my hands. Food first. Ordering in would've been easier, but I had about thirty minutes before Elena arrived. She drove to work, but she would Uber over and I would take her home. She could always get a ride with her dad in the morning. I didn't want her to be on the road late by herself. She argued it wasn't a problem. But it was a problem for me.

Her safety came first.

Opening the fridge, I pulled out ingredients for camarones al ajillo: shrimp, garlic, butter, lime, cilantro, rice, a ripe plantain, and Mamá's special seasoning. I prepped everything before the door chimed. The shrimp would go in last. Removing the pan from the heat, I wiped my hands and opened the door.

No surprises with her outfit. Black slacks, a company-branded shirt, and a messenger bag slung across her shoulder. Simple, practical, yet that outfit on her looked better than Versace on women I had dated.

Her gaze lifted, locking onto mine, then flicked to my lips.

"Planning to let me in?"

I stepped aside. As she slipped past, her body brushed mine. Heat seared through every nerve. I was a grown man; no way in hell I'd embarrass myself. Only one head controlled me, and it was the one with a brain.

She moved toward the floor-to-ceiling window, eyes sweeping over the skyline. "This place is amazing. The views. First time in a Brickell high-rise. I don't even want to imagine what you paid for this."

I smirked. "Guess I can't ask you for a loan to cover next month's mortgage."

She turned, brow lifting. "People who live in places like this don't have mortgages. They're loaded. No offense."

"None taken."

My family owned this building. I owned the one beside it. One was a known residence, the other anonymous. I'd built an underground tunnel connecting the two, an emergency escape given my line of work, though I'd used it more than once to slip out unnoticed.

Her voice cut through my thoughts. "Point me to the cutlery."

"Second drawer, opposite side of the island."

She set the island while I plated the food.

"This smells heavenly. But if you keep feeding me like this, I'm going to have to join you at the gym."

I shook my head, smiling. "You're always welcome." I set down the plates as she bowed her head to pray.

She took a bite of shrimp and moaned. A sound that sent a direct message to the wrong head. Ignoring it, I picked up my fork.

"I spoke to Nathan today. Got access to the surveillance video." How I got it wasn't a conversation I wanted to have right now.

She leaned in, spearing my last jumbo shrimp. "You must be some donor if they handed you that footage."

As she lifted it to her mouth, I moved without thinking, instincts kicking in before logic could catch up. Maybe I wanted to tease her. Maybe I wanted to see her reaction. Maybe I just wanted her. My teeth caught the shrimp just before hers, but the moment my lips skimmed hers, everything else faded. A sharp inhale. Her fingers tightened around the fork, frozen between us, as if she had forgotten what she was doing.

She stilled, breath shallow, eyes flickering with something unreadable before they drifted shut. The fork clattered onto the plate, a forgotten casualty as she leaned in.

My lips found hers, pressing in, testing. Savouring the way she softened, breath catching as her fingers brushed against my chest, then curled into my shirt as she leaned fully into the kiss. The soft hitch of surprise in her throat sent a pulse of satisfaction through me. Slow. Unrushed. Heat curled low in my stomach as I pulled back enough to take her in.

Her lips parted, cheeks flushed. Her eyes widened, stormy and searching, as if she wasn't sure whether to chase what just happened or step away. It was in the look she gave me, like her body understood before her mind could name it.

"I never thought it would feel like that."

Her words, simple and unguarded, made me smile. Being honest, I wanted to do it again and soon. My forehead rested against hers, anchoring us in the space between anticipation and surrender.

"What do you mean?" I asked, grabbing her hands to stop myself from doing something stupid with my own. Like unbuttoning her shirt and running my tongue ...

"Being kissed."

Her response stilled my thoughts.

Twenty-Eight

Bishop

I shouldn't have kissed her. Now I'm addicted. Her lips were impossibly soft. The brush of her mouth against mine sent a tingling jolt down my spine, causing the zipper of my pants to strain.

Taking a deep breath, the taste of her lingered, shrimp, with hints of garlic and lemony sauce, like she dragged the whole bite into the kiss. And I wanted a second course.

Her eyes fluttered. What did she mean when she said she never expected a kiss to feel like that? Had she imagined what it would be like to kiss me?

The faint, nearly imperceptible hum of the refrigerator blended into the quiet, its soft rhythm echoing the slow curl of Elena's fingers over mine, her warmth steady against the cool marble of the island.

Leaning back, I traced a finger down the side of Elena's face, her skin smooth and warm beneath my touch. A slow inhale parted her lips, but she kept her gaze locked on mine, unreadable yet unflinching. "I should apologize."

"Are you sorry?"

"I should be ...but I'm not. Because I want to do it again." My finger trailed down her neck. "Did the kiss live up to your fantasy?"

She leaned back, brows pulling together. "What makes you think I was fantasizing about kissing you?"

"The comment you made ..."

She shook her head. "For the record, I wasn't thinking about us kissing. Still ...I'm not sorry we did." I sat back. This wasn't a conversation to rush through. We'd crossed a line. More like erased it. I don't play games with my heart, especially after Liliana ripped it out and left me bleeding.

Elena reached forward, hesitating for a fraction of a second before her hands covered mine, as if she were second-guessing what she was about to do. Her fingers curled slightly, not quite gripping, not quite letting go. "You confuse me," she said, lifting her eyes to mine. "Everything I believed, I've started to question since spending time with you."

"Is that a bad thing?"

"I always thought I was called to be single. You know, Paul in the Bible talks about singleness and being called to serve God ..."

"But not anymore?"

She laughed, soft and uncertain. "It's not even Lent, so I can't even blame you on the devil and call you a temptation." She took a slow breath. "I'm attracted to you. At first, I thought it was just lust ... but I pride myself on being honest with myself. And the first man I've ever been attracted to ..." Her fingers tightened over mine. "Is probably the one man I shouldn't be."

I had to be honest. If there was any chance for us to move forward, to at least see where this could go, she deserved to know the truth.

Running my thumb over her hand, where she held mine, I said, "I need you to know who I've been, Elena. You've been to the Four Seasons." Keeping my eyes steady on hers, I continued, "This past year ... I lived a life I'm not proud of. But I stopped. Over a month ago now. It was empty. My body kept moving, but my soul was dead inside. I'm no saint. Maybe closer to the devil."

Her lips curved, the smile small and unsure, like a secret she wasn't ready to share. It flickered, there and gone, testing the weight of being seen. "Let's take it one day at a time. I want to get to know you. For us to know each other."

It was getting late, and we still needed a plan. But I couldn't bring myself to pull away just yet. My fingers tightened slightly around hers, lingering in this moment. Lifting her hands to my lips, I murmured, "I can do that."

Twenty-Nine

Elena

Didn't think I'd be back here so soon.

Alejandro walked me to my door last night and brushed his lips over mine. A whisper of warmth, a fleeting taste of something I couldn't name. My pulse tripped, my breath hitched, an instinct to pull him closer warred with the need to step back. Conflicted in that moment, I wanted to deepen the kiss, but I needed this – whatever it was – to move slowly.

I needed time to think.

We'd agreed, after all our talking, that he'd watch the video footage today. No way I was watching that with him, even if he asked. Instead, I offered to dig into the cremations. Never said how I planned to do it.

I pushed open the door to *Everlight Funeral Services.*

The scent of lavender and chamomile hung in the air. Soft piano music drifted from hidden speakers. Warm, recessed lighting cast a soft glow, strategically placed to eliminate harsh shadows. Plush armchairs framed a mahogany coffee table set with delicate porcelain teacups, the elegance clashing with the quiet grief lingering in the air. The decor whispered warmth and hospitality, but beneath it, loss seeped into every polished surface.

A woman in a light blue dress emerged, glancing my way. "Can I help ..." Her eyes widened with recognition, and a warm smile lit up her face. "Ms. Callos! It's so good to see you again."

"Yacena." Relief rushed through me. I'd hoped she would be here. She'd been so helpful in planning Zoë's memorial service.

Her brown eyes held a quiet question.

"Don't tell me you have another death? People rarely stop by to see me."

I shook my head, deciding to lean into the truth. I was still trying to make sense of my sister's decision.

Not a lie. "Hopefully, not anytime soon." I smiled and extended my hand, which she took.

"Let's get some coffee. Have a seat." She turned and disappeared, returning with two takeaway cups. Pointing to the teacups, she said, "Only for style. It's mostly women who come in, and we want to make the space less awkward."

I took a sip. "Wow, I need to skip the local coffee shop and come here. This is good."

"The pop of flavor is a hint of caramel and dark chocolate. Just a hint."

I savored the taste, searching for the right way to bring up the subject, but Yacena beat me to it. "Are you getting any counseling? You know our package included counseling services?"

Cradling the cup in my hands, I nodded. "Actually, when I leave here, I'm going to visit my pastor. He's a neutral sounding board."

She nodded.

I took another sip and lowered the cup. "You know, it doesn't make sense." I lifted my head, focusing on her. "We were close. Why didn't she discuss it with me?"

"Some people don't wish to burden their families." She took a sip of her coffee. "The trend now is people coming in even when they're healthy to make arrangements, to ensure their wishes are followed."

"Oh."

She crossed her feet and leaned back in the chair, coffee in hand. Death was a part of life, but she spoke about it so casually. Then again, it was her family's business. She dealt with it every day. I hoped she lived a colorful life outside these walls.

Leaning forward, I asked, "Are more people opting to be cremated?"

"Why?"

"Just wondering. I met a woman a few weeks ago whose daughter made that request. Like my family, they only found out after the daughter's death."

Glancing at her watch, she stood. "The community we serve prefers funerals. Cremations? Not as common. When we get requests," she smiled, "it's usually someone with very particular wishes. Some want their ashes taken overseas, others have more unusual requests. But it's rare."

Taking a cue from her, I hesitated, gripping my cup a little tighter. A quiet weight settled over me. This conversation hadn't given me the answers I wanted, only more questions.

Exhaling, I finally stood.

She placed a hand on my shoulder. "I hope you find peace. The sooner you accept your sister's wishes, the sooner you'll be able to move on."

Her arms touched me, a light press and release, more obligation than comfort. The warmth of human contact faded before it could settle.

"I have another meeting shortly." She stepped back, smoothing the front of her dress, fingers grazing over an unseen crease and dismissing the conversation with the same ease she brushed over her dress.

"My suggestion? Talk to your pastor. Some things are best left alone."

She pivoted on her six-inch heels, smooth but purposeful, closing a door I hadn't realized I'd opened.

Thirty

Elena

Pastor Jonas's personal assistant led me into his office. Sunlight streamed through the floor-to-ceiling windows, warming the sleek walnut floors and casting golden flecks over the sparkling waters of Biscayne Bay. Gentle ripples danced across the surface, the reflection shifting as the breeze whispered through the palm trees below. The view blurred as Yacena's words echoed in my mind. My stomach tightened, a dull ache settling beneath my ribs, each word pressing heavier than the last. Had she shut down the discussions about cremations? Or did she think I was grasping at straws? She told me to move on.

I rested my head against the cool glass. I hadn't lied about my appointment with Pastor Jonas.

Stepping toward the floating bookshelves beside the massive, U-shaped walnut executive desk, I scanned the neatly arranged volumes. No books on financial markets, despite his family managing a hedge fund worth over fifty billion dollars. It struck me every time I stepped into this office, his refusal to let the weight of wealth define him. In a world obsessed with profit margins and market trends, he anchored himself in something deeper, something eternal. Instead, Bibles in various translations lined the shelves, including *The Eliot Indian Bible (1663).* Writings from Augustine, C.S. Lewis, and Dietrich Bonhoeffer were nestled among them.

Pastor Jonas didn't collect offerings or tithes. He encouraged giving to the pantry instead, food donations rather than money. The church employed pantry staff; though, in reality, his company funded them as part of its outreach. His dedication to God and the church had always inspired me.

Framed photographs covered the walls, images of him with his brothers and parents, their expressions frozen in moments of joy and quiet strength. His father's hand rested firmly on his shoulder in one image, a silent testament to legacy. His mother's eyes shone with quiet pride in another. The warmth in those pictures contrasted with the cool precision of the office, a reminder that even in a world of numbers and power, roots and relationships still mattered. Among them were snapshots of us. Camping trips. An overseas mission to the Philippines. In one, some of the men labored over half-built houses. In another, Zoë and I grinned as we lugged electrical fittings into a new home.

He had a recent addition. A picture of Imani, himself, and me, which my dad took of us at the gala. It brought a smile to my lips. Pastor Jonas always made me and the entire church feel like one big, extended family.

No one could ever claim he was in it for the money. Giving was either to the food pantry or to other charities. But he never wanted to take one cent from his congregation. There really was no need for him to do so. He focused on giving and serving.

A low hum filled the room, drawing my gaze to the door. Pastor Jonas stepped inside, his striking green eyes landing on me. A smile took over his face.

"Elena, sorry to keep you waiting. What can I get you?" he asked, walking to his desk.

"Already had my coffee dosage for the morning. Three times a day to keep going." I checked my watch. "Not even noon yet, and I've already hit my limit."

He chuckled. "Let me call HR so we can talk about the internship placements."

This year, we agreed to offer an internship program for all young people in the congregation between sixteen and nineteen. Every business owner in the church committed to participating. Dad was taking on four interns. Any unplaced applicants would be employed by Pastor Jonas's family, either in the hedge fund or one of their other businesses.

I followed him and sat in the chair opposite his desk. Inhaling deeply, I pressed my lips together. "Don't call HR yet."

He set his phone down, brow furrowing as he walked around the desk and lowered himself into the chair beside me. "What's on your mind?" He paused, studying my face. "This is about more than the internship program. Your little worry lines are a dead giveaway."

I stared at the edge of his desk, words swimming behind my eyes. "I'm confused. So confused." My fingers twisted in my lap, nails pressing into my palm. The words hovered on the edge of my tongue, hesitation coiling tight in my chest before they finally tumbled out. "I kissed Alejandro Bishop."

His hands folded over mine, warmth seeping into my skin, grounding me. Another slow breath escaped as the weight of his touch steadied the turmoil churning inside me.

"I thought you were called to singleness. That you were dedicating your life to God, to work and ministry."

Holding his hand for strength, I said, "Honestly, so did I. That was my goal. To be content serving young people in the church."

"Do you have to be single to serve the young people?"

I hesitated. "After meeting Imani, I became fixated on not getting pregnant, knowing how much she gave up. And Dad and Mom drilled into us the sacredness of sex. I think Zoë, Zen, and I all accepted those values, even if we never said it out loud. It probably came from our religious upbringing. So, I never went on dates or had a relationship." I lifted my eyes to his. "Then one day, I realized I was twenty-five and had never even tried dating."

His grip tightened slightly offering reassurance. "But when you think of your mother, Imani, didn't God turn it all around for His glory?"

My voice caught. "At first, my commitment to purity was for all the wrong reasons. As I grew in faith, it became more than abstinence. Then watching Imani and you ... I wanted to be fully dedicated to serving God and the community."

His jaw tensed, and a shadow passed through his eyes, dimming the usual brightness. He exhaled sharply, rubbing a hand over his chin. The movement was deliberate, measured, as if weighing what to say next. The corners of his mouth twitched, like he was suppressing words he wasn't ready to speak.

"Elena." He exhaled, closing his eyes as if steadying himself. "Your example shouldn't be Imani or me. You should follow what *God* wants for you." He rose slowly, exhaling through his nose, his movements deliberate. His hands disappeared into his pockets, and something in the way he stood changed, like he was reaching inward, not just for words but for the strength to say them. "Is your call to singleness rooted in God, or fear?"

I absorbed his accusation thoughtfully.

He leaned against his desk, crossing his arms over his chest, his fingers drumming absently against his sleeve as he watched me. "Sometimes, we hide behind God."

Thirty-One

Bishop

The faint sizzle of something searing on the teppanyaki grill carried over from the open kitchen, punctuated by the occasional hiss of steam and the deep, rich aroma of soy sauce and charred beef.

In between reviewing and signing off on disbursements the foundation needed to make, I went over the footage. I even sent it to Drago. He came to the same verdict: a professional hit disguised as a mugging-gone-wrong.

My phone vibrated.

Elena.

Five minutes away.

The surrounding voices faded as I replayed the footage in my mind. The attacker came from the left. Smooth and controlled like a shadow breaking free from the alley. Paula had no time to react.

Two strides.

One hand shot out, clamping over her mouth. A sharp twist of her neck.

Quick.

Efficient.

Professional.

Then he emptied her bag, scattering the contents enough to sell the illusion of a mugging. The mark of a professional. He knew every camera angle and tried to avoid them all.

A black mask covered his face, a blot of red staining the front. Not Paula's blood, for sure.

This was a professional hit.

But why?

Elena uncovered something dangerous, dangerous enough for someone to kill over. We needed a new plan. I shifted in my seat, the stiff chair forcing me to sit straight. Slouch, and I'd be on the floor.

How the hell was I supposed to tell her this?

She appeared the moment I thought of her, striding toward me like fate had set the timing. The moment she came into view, some of the weight on my shoulders lifted, just a little. I couldn't wait for her to be next to me. I didn't want to share what Drago and I had uncovered about Paula's death. But I had to.

As she made her way to the table, our eyes met and a warm, involuntary grin stretched across my face. I loved her effortless style. Elena never dressed to impress, never swayed her hips to demand attention, but those black pants accentuated every curve. She didn't put herself on display. She was something rare, meant to be unwrapped in private by one, not ogled by many.

Hopefully, that "one" was me.

She slid into the seat beside me, placing her bag down. "We need to stop meeting like this."

"After a day of reviewing that video, I welcomed the chance to feed you." I rested my hand on hers. "Plus, I'm removing temptation." Raising her hand to my lips, I smirked. "Because after tasting you, believe me, I'm no saint. And honestly? I want another course."

She arched a brow, a smirk tugging at the corners of her lips. "Tell me that's not your version of sweet talk. Women actually fall for that?"

"You wound me."

The waiter approached with quiet grace, dressed in a crisp black kimono-style jacket. A deep indigo apron, neatly tied at the waist, contrasted against the traditional white tabi socks and black zori sandals that glided over the polished wooden floor.

As soon as he took our order, Elena turned to me. "What did you find?"

"You first," I suggested, hoping to stall in sharing the findings. It was inevitable, but I didn't want to put a bigger cloud over our evening, given what we were discussing.

"The funeral home didn't yield much." She took a sip of water. "But when I asked if there'd been an increase in cremations, her answer was ... off." Her brows drew together. "Up until then, the conversation had been smooth. I don't know. Maybe I'm overthinking."

Maybe not. Everlight Funeral Services may need a closer look.

"What about you?" she asked.

The waiter returned with our starters, buying me a few seconds. I set down my glass. "Don't eat yet. I don't want you choking." Resting my eyes on hers, "Paula's death was staged as a mugging. But it was a professional hit," I confessed.

She pulled back, a brow arching. "And you figured this out how?"

"Just trust me."

Then suddenly, slithering toward me was a serpent wrapped in elegance. Her handler trailed behind, devious and complicit. My mind screamed for them to keep walking. For their own good, keep walking.

She might be the snake, but I was the predator that hunted them. Nothing had provoked me to strike, yet.

She stopped at the table, eyes flicking over Elena disdainfully. "Bishop," she purred. "It's so good to see you. My boss and I are here for a quick dinner. You should call sometime."

"Liliana." I leaned back, letting the ice in my voice do the work. "Pretend we never met."

Elena turned to me, her expression unreadable. "You know, this lobster is delicious. We wouldn't want it to go cold."

Jameson moved past her and wormed his way toward their table. When I glanced over my shoulder, his focus wasn't on Liliana. He stared straight at us.

More precisely, at Elena.

Hell no.

My fingers drummed once against the table, slow and deliberate. My eyes pinned him to the spot. Then, I smirked, watching him sit. Let him feel me watching him.

Forget about ruining his political career even before it even starts...I'd end *him*.

Thirty-Two

Elena

A steaming bowl of ramen. Bishop's gorgeous lips. Soft kisses trailing along my jaw, lower, down my neck ...

A shrill flute note slashed through my dream, ripping me from the cocoon of sleep. A jolt of adrenaline shot through me, my pulse spiking as my breath hitched in my throat.

I bolted upright, blinking to clear sleep from my eyes. That alarm signal came from Dad's house. The phone showed 2:35 a.m. This early in the morning, it wasn't a drill. I dashed to the safe in the back of my closet and pulled out the gun. Zen trained both Zoë and me, drilling us in self-defense and emergency response for moments like this.

My phone vibrated on the bedside table.

Zeno's name flashed across the screen. He spoke in a measured tone, "The police are on their way."

"I'm going over."

"Stay put until they get there. They cut the video feed inside the house."

"Zen, I'm not staying here. I need to check on Dad."

"If you step out there and get yourself killed, I'll never forgive you."

"Love you, too."

"Don't hang up. Put on something with a pocket and keep the phone on you."

I yanked a button-down shirt from the laundry basket and shoved the phone into the pocket. I skipped the shoes; less noise that way.

Racing to Dad's house, I clicked off the safety on the gun. My heartbeat thundered, every beat slamming against my ribs. I'm certain the force must have cracked at least two. The moon cast long shadows over the deserted street, the cool night air sharp against my skin. The stillness pressed in. If anyone was still inside Dad's house, they could probably hear my heartbeat hammering.

"The door is ajar. Can you hear me?" I whispered.

Peering inside, my knees buckled, a wave of dizziness threatening to take me down. The dim glow of a single overturned lamp flickered against the wall casting jagged shadows over the chaos, chairs were toppled, a vase shattered, and the acrid scent of something metallic hung in the air. What the hell? Nothing like this ever happened here.

Sirens wailed in the distance. I shouldn't go in. This was clearly a crime scene ... but I needed to find Dad.

"I'm going in. I can hear the police sirens."

"Ellieee," he whisper-called my name, pleading with me to wait. If Zen were here, he would not have waited. This was the man who took me in and raised me. He didn't have to, but he chose to.

No, I could not wait.

Stepping into the house, I wished I had put on shoes as I tried to dodge the shards of ceramic from the shattered vase.

Then I saw something. At the dining room table. My gun remained aimed and ready. I flipped the light switches for the kitchen and dining room areas.

"Zen."

"What is it, Ellie?"

My throat clenched. A scream caught behind my lips. Tears welled in my eyes, blurring my vision as I tried to process the scene before me. A sob escaped. "Zen ... no ... Oh gosh ... Dad is tied to a chair."

Thirty-Three

Bishop

When the call connected, Drago's voice came through. "Bishop."

"I just sent you details of Elena's dad's home address."

"What's going on, man?" Drago asked.

I sped toward the hospital, willing to pay every ticket with a tip. The engine growled as I pushed past empty intersections, the occasional streetlight flickering against the deserted roads. Miami at this hour was abandoned, the silence pressing in except for the hum of my tires gripping the asphalt.

The city stretched around me, and neon signs reflected off the damp pavement as I raced past storefronts. All I could focus on was getting to her. My grip tightened on the wheel, my jaw locked. The idea of her being in danger set my nerves on fire. I had seen violence before, too much of it, but this?

This was personal. Personal for me.

Elena's sobs still echoed in my ear, my grip tightening on the steering wheel. I'd filled Drago in on her dad's attack and asked him to pull the security feed. Hopefully, something useful was recorded before it was cut. He promised results within the hour. The system was probably low-tech, so I expected his call back within minutes.

I pushed through the hospital doors. Overhead came a page for a trauma team. Nurses walked briskly along the corridor; an orderly wheeled someone past. Even in the chaos of it all, that sterile hospital smell still hit me, sharp, cold, and impossible to name, a mix of antiseptic and a good dose of fear.

Hospitals have always carried a sense of unease for me. Too many bad memories. Too many nights waiting with Dad and Mom when my sister was admitted to hospital.

When I reached the floor and room Elena had told me in her message, I lightly knocked before pushing the door open. The beeping of heart monitors and the faint murmur of nurses at the station outside filled the room. The sharp tang of disinfectant clung to the air.

She stood wrapped in Imani's arms. Pastor Jonas sat, leaning forward with his elbows on his knees. Everyone stared at Theo, lying motionless on the bed. The silence in the room was thick, broken only by the soft beeping of machines.

When my eyes connected with Elena's, she broke away from Imani and rushed toward me. Relief slammed into me like a tidal wave. I hadn't realized how badly I needed to see her standing, breathing, whole.

In that moment, I was like a man pulled from the wreckage, bruised, shaken, but alive and clutching the only thing that mattered.

I kissed her forehead, and she mumbled into my neck, "None of this makes any sense."

She lifted her eyes to mine. "The police will be back later this morning." A shudder coursed through her, and her grip tightened on my shirt as she steadied herself. "They told Dad to press the silent alarm, or they'd come to my house and shoot me. He had fallen asleep in the family room watching television." She stopped and wet her lips. "They placed him in the chair. To save me... he pressed it. That was the last thing before they knocked him out." Shaking her head, she whispered again, "None of this makes any sense."

I held her as she walked back to Imani. My gut twisted. Her shoulders stayed high and stiff while she leaned into me. I wished I could erase her fears and concerns. Her bottom lip trembled before she bit it, trapping the shake.

Pastor Jonas stood and rested a hand on my shoulder. His touch was firm and steady, meant to comfort, but I couldn't shake the tension coiled in my chest. I wasn't used to this comfort, this reassurance he offered. It was like armor not quite my size; it clung awkwardly, unfamiliar and stiff. We sat and waited for an update on Theo.

An hour ticked by. Still no call from Drago. What was taking so long?

Elena's phone vibrated. She answered and updated the person on the other end. I assumed it was her brother, Zeno, since she called him 'Zen.' The conversation turned heated.

Her brows pinched together as she kept speaking to him. It was clear they were arguing about Theo and her safety.

"Zen, we don't know what this is. If you want Dad to come to Etim, fine. But with Zoë gone, I have to stay and run the business. We still have projects." She fell silent, listening to him.

Leaning in, I murmured, "Let me talk to him."

Taking the phone, I walked out of earshot. "Zeno, this is Bishop. Co-owner of Baas International."

"You're kidding me," he responded.

"I don't joke about things like that. If Elena wants to stay, I'll protect her. She'll be safe."

"What are you to Ellie?"

"It's ... complicated."

"Complicated? Co-owner of Baas or not, if she stays and gets hurt, I will personally hunt you down and kill you myself."

Something told me he would try. Only try. But if I ever hurt Elena, I would let him kill me. I would hand him a suppressed SIG, along with every weapon in my house. The secured vault held everything from tactical gear to a black-market RPG, compact enough to sling across a shoulder but loud enough to end a convoy. Drago would have a stroke if he ever found out what I kept tucked away. In our field, you could never be too prepared.

"Someone just hacked into Dad's home security. It alerted me five minutes after the fact."

"That's my partner."

Zeno rattled off why hacking in was impossible. His system combined AI-driven encryption, biometric voice recognition, and a two-factor authenticator that refreshed at randomized intervals, all protected by layered firewalls and real-time anomaly detection.

No wonder Drago took longer than usual. His system was solid. Ours was just better.

Down the corridor, the doctor stepped out. He adjusted his glasses, his face unreadable as he headed toward Elena. "A doctor's approaching her. Listen, I need to wrap this up before Elena reclaims her phone. Once your father is cleared to be released, I will personally put him on my private plane and get him to you safely."

I ended the call and strode toward her, every step tightening the knot in my gut. No matter what it took, I would make sure she never had to live with this kind of fear again.

First order of the day: Get Elena a new encrypted phone and move her the hell out of her place. The thought of her being vulnerable in that house made my blood burn. Someone had crossed a line, and I wasn't about to sit back and wait for them to try again. Protecting her wasn't a duty, it was personal now. Whatever we stumbled into, they went out of their way to send a message.

I planned on doing a return to sender.

Thirty-Four

Elena

The elevator door slid open into Alejandro's apartment. Must be nice to have an entire floor to yourself.

After much debate, Zen gave me two options. I could get on the plane with Dad and leave everything behind, or I could stay with Alejandro, knowing we still did not understand what we were up against.

Each option presented its own challenge. One meant running and damaging our business reputation. The other meant trusting a man I did not fully understand. Neither option was ideal, but staying with Alejandro made more sense.

Zeno called him Bishop ... for some strange reason, I'm the only one who calls him by his first name.

Imani wanted me to stay with her. Mrs. Sinclair, Pastor Jonas' mother, even called, offering me a place with their family. Their compound sprawled over several acres, each family member with their own private residence and the main home belonging to his parents. Every year, they hosted our church's Christmas party, and over a hundred people attended.

For reasons only he knew, Zeno shut that down. I liked Mrs. Sinclair. Pastor Jonas had pressed his lips into a tight line, his brows drawing together, when Zeno said no. There was a flicker of something unreadable in his eyes. Disappointment, maybe frustration. He even offered to hire security if that made Zen more comfortable. Pastor Jonas stepped away and spoke to Zen on the phone, and afterwards, somehow, he agreed that I should stay with Alejandro.

So here I was, stepping into his home for an indefinite period, at least until the police figured something out. Or until Zen and Alejandro decided it was safe for Dad and me to return home.

My hands clenched the strap of my bag, knuckles aching. A cold weight pressed against my chest, my breath shallow and unsteady. No amount of pretending could erase the tremor in my fingers or the sick churn in my gut. The image of Dad, tied to that chair, his head limp against his chest, seared itself into my mind. And it wouldn't fade anytime soon. If ever.

But what haunted me most was that they would have come over to my house and shot me if he hadn't sounded the alarm.

I didn't understand. Why us? We'd won some big contracts for a medium-sized company. Could this be one of our competitors?

Alejandro carried my flute and large suitcase, but I held on to my carry-on. In that moment, it served two purposes: It was one of the few choices still under my control and it was something to steady myself with. My body was ready to give out.

I smiled to myself. I could really use a laugh right now. I thought about Christmas movies where women packed a week's supply of ball gowns and outfits into one carry-on. Somehow, I didn't have that grace. The Hallmark Channel should offer a packing course.

Alejandro stepped in behind me, resting a hand on the small of my back. "Staying here is for the best."

I was too tired to argue.

"Your room is next to mine. Connected by an adjoining door. You can lock it or leave it open." He slowed, forcing me to stop and turn toward him. His voice was even, casual, like we were discussing my day at the office.

"If they get in ... they won't get back out."

What the hell? A chill snaked down my spine, every nerve on high alert. Did he just say that? His tone hadn't changed, but something in the air had a sharp edge, a quiet warning. I searched his face for a tell, but he gave nothing away. I was missing something.

He nodded for me to keep going down the hall.

We passed a full-length pool and a gym with floor-to-ceiling glass overlooking the water. Then, and only then, did we reach the bedrooms.

Five! Who needs five bedrooms when they live alone?

"This one's mine."

A few more steps. Maybe twenty. Then my door. He pushed it open, and we stepped inside.

A king-size bed sat against a sleek wood-paneled wall, the crisp white linens untouched. The room carried the cool hush of a space rarely used. A low-profile seating area faced the windows, city lights reflecting off polished floors.

I exhaled, the quiet opulence pressing in.

He gestured ahead. "Through here are the closet and bathroom." A closet big enough to park two twenty-foot containers.

An en suite bathroom. A deep soaking tub sat beneath another massive window. The city stretched beyond, buzzing and alive.

I peered over my shoulder. "Shucks. Forgot to bring my crown."

His hand returned to the small of my back. "And here I thought humility was your strong suit."

I looked up at him with a small smile. The shift was instant. His expression hollowed and jaw tightened, like someone had cut the power to him. His shoulders tensed, his stance shifted as if bracing for something unseen.

"I know you're tired. But we need to talk."

Thirty-Five

Elena

I walked into the kitchen, greeted by the buttery scent of eggs and the sharp tang of feta dancing in the warm air. Alejandro stood at the stove, the gentle sizzle of cooking omelets filling the quiet as he folded crumbles of cheese into the pan with practiced ease.

Washing my hands at the sink, I asked, "How can I help?"

"Salad is in the fridge. Garlic bread is in the oven. It can come out now."

I pulled the garlic bread from the oven, the heat warming my fingertips through the oven mitt as the buttery, garlicky aroma hit me full force. I set the tray on the island, the bread crust crackling as it settled. I'd lived on my own for three years now, all of them spent in the same gated community as my family. Being in Alejandro's house should've been strange, but it wasn't. Maybe because we spent so much time together over the past few weeks.

With Pastor Jonas and his family, I knew I would have been safe. Still, Zen insisted I stay with Alejandro. The possibility of that person returning to our area was highly unlikely. But until the police said otherwise, I wasn't foolish enough to test the theory. Maybe I read too many books or watched one too many true crime documentaries. Slim chance or not, it only took one mistake. I wasn't about to make that mistake.

The scent of chives and onions pulled me back. Rich, warm, and mouthwatering, it stirred something comforting in me, along with a sudden wave of hunger. Alejandro set my plate in front of me, then took his seat with his own. The steam coming off the plates lingered between us, and the low murmur of the news on the television filled the background. But it was his quiet presence, steady and attentive, that filled the space as he waited for me to bless the food.

I hated cold eggs, so this wasn't the time for conversation.

His gaze lingered on me. I turned. He smirked.

I finished my prayer and promptly stuck a forkful of eggs into my mouth.

He laughed. "Good, huh?"

"Don't want my food to get cold," I mumbled behind another mouthful

He laughed and followed my lead.

I picked the avocado out of my salad.

"You can't be serious," he questioned. "Who doesn't like avocado?"

I shrugged.

He reached over with his fork and stole the slices from my plate, grinning like a thief who knew he'd get away with it.

"Finished?" he asked, pushing his empty plate aside.

I nodded cheerfully. "FYI, it was delicious. Thank you."

I pushed back my chair to clear the plates, but he stopped me. The playfulness on his face faded, replaced by something sharper. His gaze locked on mine, dissecting every flicker of emotion, like he needed to memorize the shape of my soul.

"I know you would've preferred to stay with Pastor Jonas."

I didn't need to nod. Pastor Jonas was more than a mentor. He always listened. Not only to me, to everyone. He would've built a fortress around me if he had to.

"Zeno knows something about me that most people don't." He rested a hand on my left hand, which was on the island. "Your brother isn't a fool. He's aware that the attack on your father was a message."

"A message? For Zen?" He could be ruthless in business. Some believed he walked with one foot in the underworld, dealing with men whose power came from more than just boardrooms and balance sheets. Men with blood ties and buried secrets. Mafia.

He threaded his fingers through mine. "No. It was a message to you."

Some part of my mind had already been toying with the idea that, somehow, I'd placed my dad in danger. But hearing it spoken aloud made the guilt infinitely worse. A hollow thud echoed in my chest. I couldn't breathe for a second, like someone knocked the air out of me. *What if this really was my fault?* A tremor passed through my free arm. My palm pressed flat to the cool underside of the counter, grounding me.

I leaned back, taking in his face. "What does Zen know about you?"

"Southshore Memorial didn't hand over Kellie's report. And I never got Paula's video from Nathan Carmichael."

I swallowed hard, eyes fixed on him.

"What I do ..." He looked down, jaw tight. "Think special forces. Only quieter. Off the books. Government ghosts."

His eyes, already dark, deepened. He reached out, brushed a loose strand from my messy bun, and tucked it behind my ear. His fingers trailed lightly against my skin, warm and deliberate, sending a subtle current across my cheek.

"And I have no problem using those skills to keep you safe."

A question pressed at the edge of my lips. But I wasn't stupid.

When I was small, I thought spies only existed in movies. Until Dad took us on a trip to Virginia. The tour operator pointed out, from the road, where the CIA headquarters sat, tucked away and hidden. We couldn't see it. But I was five, and that moment made the movies real. My pulse kicked. How was I supposed to process this?

No wonder Zen wanted me here.

Alejandro Bishop was a spy, or something of the sort. At the very least.

Thirty-Six

Bishop

Tying my sneakers, I mulled over my conversation with Elena last night. She was a real trooper; she took everything in stride. Some part of me expected her to freak out... faint maybe, when I shared a little about my real line of work. But she didn't. She simply got up from the island and washed the plates. I stood there, tension tight in my shoulders, listening to the quiet clink of dishes. Maybe that was how she processed things, quietly, inwardly. When she was finished, she went to bed.

I stretched. A thirty-minute run before my sparring partner arrived was exactly what my body needed. It was just after five. With Elena safely here and her dad in Etim, I finally had a puzzle to start piecing together.

I pushed open my bedroom door and stopped. A slow, mournful melody slipped into the hallway and lodged itself in my chest. Elena played what she couldn't say, and it hit harder than words ever could.

Beautiful, yet laced with sadness

The melody trailed behind me as I walked down the hall and into the gym. It clung to me with a weight I couldn't shake. Turning on the treadmill, I tried to outrun it, but I couldn't.

Even when my sparring partner arrived, I couldn't focus. We called six time-outs in twenty minutes. After a kick landed too hard, he doubled over, and I knew we had to stop. The last thing I wanted was to injure him.

Those notes from Elena's flute gave me a glimpse into her soul. What she couldn't say in words, she poured into that instrument. And it wrecked me.

Under the shower, the melody still echoed in my head. Forget the puzzle. Today, we needed to take a break. We could do whatever she wanted. A trip to see the Eiffel Tower or the Leaning Tower of Pisa. Sail the River Thames. Stand all day at Buckingham Palace to watch the guards change. Anything.

I stepped into the kitchen, a plan forming. Fruit already sat on the island.

"Morning," she greeted, her smile warm but dimmed at the edges. "Saw you working out," she added. "So breakfast is fruit with Greek yogurt, topped with granola. Also, grilled ham and feta cheese sandwiches with a side salad."

I leaned in and inhaled. "I could get used to this."

"Don't," she said, a teasing smile tugging at her lips. "But it's the least I could do." Her eyes met mine. "Thank you for being honest with me."

I reached for her, my fingers grazing her jawline. "One thing you can be certain about, I'll always be honest with you." I brushed a kiss across her lips. "Come. Let's eat."

After she blessed the meal, I picked up a spoonful of yogurt. "I want to make a suggestion. Let's forget everything for one day. You can do whatever you want. The plane is already on standby."

She cut her sandwich, two halves into four triangles. Her smile lit up her entire face, eyes gleaming like they held their own private sunrise. "Anything? We can do anything?"

I nodded, already suspecting I might live to regret it.

When we boarded a hop-on hop-off bus from Bayside Marketplace, I knew this wasn't my idea of a good time. Why couldn't she have picked the Leaning Tower of Pisa?

She handed me earphones.

"How many times have you done this tour?"

She smiled. "Zoë and I loved to play tourist. I've lost count. Sometimes we'd skip some stops, but we always got off at Wynwood." She added, "You?"

Smiling down at her, I said, "First time. You know all of this is within driving distance of where we live?"

"There's no fun in that. I love watching tourists fall in love with our city."

When we reached Lincoln Road, she announced, "Let's get off there."

We got off at the Lincoln Road stop, and I laced our fingers together as we strolled along the avenue, stopping to buy ice cream. I had to admit, it was relaxing. She chose a cone, and I went with a cup.

No schedule.

Nowhere to be.

The heat bounced off the pavement, and the breeze barely cut through the sun's intensity. The creamy sweetness of the ice cream melted fast, running down her fingers. She laughed and licked it up before it could reach her wrist, and I couldn't look away.

And then a familiar face from the not-so-distant past walked toward me. Her hand was linked with a young man's, and even from here, I could see a twinkling in her eyes. She paused when she recognized me, said something to him, and after placing a kiss on his lips, rushed over.

She glanced at Elena. I gave a small nod. "You can speak in front of her. She knows."

"You were right," she said. "I want to thank you for your honesty. I would've regretted it. And I would never have met Xavier."

"Rox—"

"Tania," she cut me off. "That's my real name." She turned to Elena. "He's a good man."

Then she returned to her boyfriend, hooking her arm into his. Seeing her happy brought a measure of satisfaction. During that dark time, at least once, I'd put someone else before me.

I placed a kiss on Elena's cheek, treasuring her even more right then. We continued walking as I told her about the turning point that made me walk away from the dark path I had taken. In the process, it seemed like I helped Tania avoid the same mistake.

Spotting a street artist, I pointed in their direction. I wanted to capture this day. I sat, pulling her gently onto my lap, our heads resting together.

"You know this sketch will be a hundred bucks," the artist said.

"I'll give you five hundred if you personally drop it off at my home. I don't want it to get damaged."

"You're serious, man?"

I pulled out a business card, along with two hundred-dollar bills, and promised him the concierge at the front desk would give him the balance on delivery.

We sat, resting our heads together. Then I turned and looked at her. Our eyes met, steady and unblinking. The hum of the street around us faded, replaced by the quiet thrum of something unspoken. There was a pull between us, magnetic and warm, like the moment before a storm breaks but without the ensuing chaos. I couldn't describe the feeling, even if I tried. In that moment, three words formed in my throat. I didn't say them. Obviously. But when the artist finished and I studied the drawing, the words I hadn't spoken were right there on the page.

Could she see what the artist captured? I hoped not.

But Elena wasn't a fool; that's what I liked about her.

Only a few hours ago, I'd promised to be honest with her. First, I needed to be honest with myself.

Thirty-Seven

Bishop

The whiskey slid smoothly down my throat, with a smoky heat that lingered at the back of my mouth, a whisper of burn at the end. The Miami skyline stretched out in front of me. We reached home about three hours ago. Dinner at Bayside Marketplace, then ended the night on the Skyviews Wheel.

Elena could've asked for anything, anywhere, but she chose something quiet. Unpretentious. She didn't need anything flashy. That's what I loved about her. She didn't need things to make her happy; she loved a simple life.

And I loved her.

I hadn't said the words. My love for her had crept in. Or maybe I'd always known, there was something different about her from the moment I saw her in the elevator. I couldn't deny it, even if I wanted to. It was lodged now in my subconscious ... in my heart ... etched into the very core of my soul.

I loved her quick wit, her fierce loyalty. Even when her peace was at stake and everything was falling apart, her quiet, unshakable faith, remained steady.

Okay ... I loved a lot of things about her.

I gripped the tumbler of whiskey tighter. As sure as I was that the ice would melt in this glass, I was even surer that I was in love with Elena. It almost slipped out on Lincoln Road. With everything going on, she wasn't ready to hear those words.

My sister would've loved her. Maybe I should introduce her to my parents.

I paused on the way to the kitchen. Maybe not. My mom might scare her off by pulling up bridal sites five minutes in. I should pour another whiskey since sleep wasn't going to happen. But it was almost midnight, and technically, that meant I'd gone a whole day without working.

I grabbed my laptop from the office and poured another drink. Elena's comment about Yacena stuck in my head. That shift in her behavior when Elena mentioned cremations ...

Since sleep was still dodging me, I might as well be productive.

Twenty-seven minutes. That's how long it took me to get into Yacena's system. I should've gone straight for her records, but Drago and I always followed the money. Money talks. And sometimes it screams.

I hit a second firewall. Nothing I hadn't seen before, but it meant someone didn't want this trail followed. I cracked through in ten minutes.

It took another two hours to piece things together. I traced a trail of transactions, routing codes, encrypted spreadsheets, buried metadata and found two offshore accounts tied to her. Not the business. Her. One in the Caymans. One in Malta. Both receiving monthly deposits.

I couldn't see exact balances, but the pattern was clear. Those accounts held millions.

I made coffee, not that I needed the caffeine tonight. My system was already wired. But stepping away from the screen to make the coffee gave me time to think.

Why was someone, or more likely, several someones, funneling that kind of money into her accounts?

The deposits came from two different companies. Smart move. They were offshore too. But I had been in this game long enough to know most identities behind those companies were buried deep. Almost bottomless. *Almost.* Given time, I could trace them.

I switched to an easier task and pulled up Yacena's financial records.

Soft footsteps padded across the hardwood floor, followed by the faint rustle of fabric. A hint of vanilla and something citrusy drifted toward me. Her presence stirred the air before I even turned around.

"Why are you up?" I asked, eyes still locked to my computer

"You should ask yourself that," she said, voice soft, still thick with sleep. "I wanted water. Forgot to bring a bottle in with me."

She came to stand beside me, hand resting on my shoulder. "You know it's after three?"

"Your comment about Yacena nagged at me."

"And?"

"She's not just doing well from the business, she lied." I pointed to the screen. "Their cremation numbers *are* up over the last twelve months. Most of their referrals are coming from Southshore Memorial and St. Andrews."

Elena pulled up a chair beside me. Her voice dropped. "Dad was attacked the same night I visited her. Any chance it's connected?"

I switched screens. The accounts made one thing clear. Yacena was offering more than funeral services.

Thirty-Eight

Elena

So much swirled in my mind. Dad's attack. My deepening feelings for Alejandro. And that she lied to me. The woman who stood and helped us plan every aspect of my sister's memorial service lied to me.

Lord, just one more day to breathe would have helped. But the weight of responsibility didn't pause for reflection or grief. With Dad in Etim, five hours ahead, and the reins temporarily in my hands, stepping away wasn't even an option. I was already behind before I even started. I had no illusions about being totally in charge. By the time I opened my laptop, Etim's morning had already unfolded, and five emails from Dad waited for me like an ambush. One was a link inviting the senior team members to a meeting in an hour.

I didn't mind. With everything going on, having Dad still keeping a pulse on the business was a relief. I knew it helped him stay occupied and kept him from dwelling on the attack. And deep down, I also knew he didn't want to burden me.

I ordered fruit cups and apple muffins from the café across the road for the meeting. After Dad's call, I planned to hold a projects meeting to get a real-time status update. We updated our project management system daily, but brainstorming together always sparked better solutions. It was an inside joke around here that the best ideas are born over spilled coffee and loud debates. We're proof that collective chaos can spark brilliance.

Seeing Dad on the conference call made tears sting the back of my eyes. We hadn't told anyone about the attack. Watching him command the meeting, it was hard to believe that four days ago he'd been pistol-whipped, tied to a chair, and left unconscious. Gratitude and fury wrestled inside me. Somehow, fury was winning. How dare someone do that to him? Dad wouldn't hurt a soul. Lord, if Yacena was involved, may she pay for her sins.

After Dad signed off, everyone provided updates. Mark mentioned he still hadn't heard from the hospice project and reminded us about his family reunion next month, ten days on a European cruise with his big family. Mark's a good guy. I prayed one day he would find a good woman. Zoë would've wanted that for him too. She always said Mark had the kind of heart you build a future with.

I returned to my office to finalize a closeout report to accompany an invoice, incorporating the edits the team suggested during the meeting. The phone on my desk rang. My admin assistant said a Ms. Ortega was in the reception area to see me. She didn't have an appointment but wanted a brief meeting about possibly hiring us for work at her company.

We needed to hire another engineer, especially with Zoë... I pressed the heels of my hands to my eyes, trying to stop the tears building at the thought of her. With Dad gone and Zoë not here, the team needed support. But I didn't have space for one more thing on my to-do list.

Still, turning away a potential client without even hearing her out, even if she hadn't made an appointment, was wrong.

When the admin assistant brought her in, I stood. At the sight of her, my brows drew together instinctively. She walked in like she owned the place. Heels clicked against the floor. Her eyes swept the room, as if measuring my worth by the thread count on the chairs. What was she playing at? I looked past her and nodded at my assistant. "Thank you."

"I'd extend my hand, but I'm not sure you'd take it," the woman said, settling into the seat opposite me and resting her designer bag in the chair beside her.

The night she stopped at our table during dinner, I hadn't really gotten a good look at her. Now I could see she was stunning and clearly had a far better sense of fashion than I ever would. She flipped her long, glossy black hair over her right shoulder.

"Liliana, right?"

A slow, deliberate smile stretched across her lips, not warm, not kind, but calculated. "Guess he told you about me."

"Not really. We've been busy. You came by our table the other night at dinner."

Her smile twisted into a smirk.

"Like I said," I continued. "I'm busy. And you're not here to ask our company to do work for you."

"Do you really know Bishop?" she asked, sitting back and crossing her legs, like the chair belonged to her.

"Tell me why you're here again."

"You seem like a nice girl. Not his type."

Raising a brow, I countered with "Should I assume by your comment, then, that you're not a nice girl?" She picked the wrong office, the wrong woman, and the wrong day. I'd spent years on construction sites brushing off men who mistook my silence for submission. Her scare tactics? Amateur hour.

"Well, I didn't know at the time..." She paused, eyes skimming the room, dissecting every corner of my space as if taking mental inventory of the details she could later weaponize. "He prefers hookups." Her lips curled as she leaned in and whispered, "How else can I say it? He's a manwhore."

I stood, walked to the door, and opened it. With a smile fixed on my face, I said, "Thank God for the cross."

She blinked, surprised. I held the door open wider.

Thirty-Nine

Bishop

I leaned forward, biting into my pizza. The crust crackled between my teeth, still warm, the flavor bursting with the tang of tomato sauce, the salt of pepperoni, and a touch of smoky char. What the—

Glass reformed. Tires screeched backward. A bullet leapt from cracked metal back into the barrel of the gun.

Did that scene just happen in reverse? No wonder Drago recommended this movie.

My eyes narrowed. Completely unrealistic. But man, the cinematography was next level. Something about watching time unravel reminded me of those missions where cause and consequence blurred, and we knew the ending before we even started.

Inversion theory didn't bother me. I'd lived it in ops where the past shaped the future before the mission even began.

Elena messaged earlier. I told her tonight was about relaxing. Whatever she wanted to watch was fine by me.

Soft amber light spilled into the home cinema, breaking the shadows that clung to the leather recliners and soundproof walls. It cut through the dimness like a quiet intrusion, warm and slow, and pulled my attention toward the door.

I turned my head as Elena dropped into the seat beside me and grabbed a slice of pizza.

She pointed at the screen. "Watch this part."

Onscreen, a car skidded across a rain-slicked street, backward, then shot forward again as if time hiccupped. The protagonist sprinted through chaos, ducking behind debris that flew in reverse.

"This is where it starts to make sense," she added. "If you've been paying attention."

"You've seen it?"

"We do family movie night twice a year. Big deal. This was my pick last year."

I leaned in and kissed her, wanting to linger ... but I pulled back. I grabbed another slice of pizza to keep my hands and mouth occupied.

Eyes on the screen, I asked, "How was your day?"

She rested her head on my shoulder. "Let's watch the movie."

Her head tilted up as I looked down. I leaned closer. She reached up and wrapped her arms around my neck. The movie faded into the background.

Elena, soft and yielding in my arms, took center stage.

Her breath warmed my neck, slow and steady, as we kissed. She smelled like herself. Worn cotton, a trace of lotion, and the kind of warmth that lingers after a long day. No perfume. Just her. Real. Unfiltered.

I pulled away for a moment. Forehead to hers, I murmured, "I'm going to yield not to temptation."

She raised a brow. "Somebody knows the Bible."

"Yup. Also—'Jesus wept.' My favorite verse in Sunday school. I wasn't always lost."

She shook her head, smiling. "Speaking of that... I had a visitor today. Someone concerned about me because of your reputation."

Her finger traced my jawline. "You've got a nice jaw."

Did she really drop that bomb and expect me to stay chill?

My jaw tensed. No part of me wanted Elena to be tangled in the wreckage of my past.

Who the hell visited her? Jonas? Imani? Mark? Each had a reason to be protective. But I wasn't that man anymore. The truth was, I never really had been. Just a guy in free fall, lying to himself.

She tugged loosely at her messy bun, and thick curls tumbled down her back, brushing my arm. They smelled like honey and peppermint, the kind of scent that makes you lean in without thinking. Her curls slid through my fingers, soft and familiar, centering me in a way I hadn't expected. She pressed her lips to my jaw, warm, lingering, full of quiet intent, and my breath caught. Her touch didn't ask. It didn't demand. A slow burn moved through my chest, spreading beneath my skin as she nestled her head against me like I was home.

"So?" I asked.

"Can you promise not to disturb this peace?"

"Tell me."

"You haven't promised."

My hand slid down her back. She wiggled under my touch.

I didn't have to play fair. I never made promises I couldn't keep.

"Maybe I should find all the places you're ticklish."

She punched my shoulder. "Not fair."

I laughed. I wouldn't have actually tickled her, but the threat worked. She softened.

"Liliana."

I pushed her up gently so I could see her face.

"Told you it'd wreck our zen. Or whatever the young people say."

She recounted the unpleasant visit, without going into any dramatics as some women would do. She stuck to the facts.

Liliana? Why would she show up at Elena's office? Maybe it was time I paid her a visit.

For all her noise, she never knew why I ended things. Never saw the photos. Never saw herself, on her knees, crawling back to her married boss.

One thing was clear. Liliana didn't come to warn Elena out of some noble instinct. This had Jameson Wakefield written all over it.

I remembered the way his eyes lingered on Elena at the restaurant. There was nothing casual about it. He stared a little too long, a little too interested. Like he was already calculating what it would take to peel her away.

What the hell was he up to?

No. Rather what were they up to?

Forty

Bishop

Liliana's visit to Elena left me unsettled, making me cut my workout short. I only did cardio, skipping resistance training, Jaden and Drago would say I was slacking off. In our field, being in top physical shape was nonnegotiable.

After showering, I threw on jeans and a T-shirt, ready to spend the day snooping into Jameson Wakefield. I'd also be sending Liliana a little gift of my own.

Elena walked into the kitchen already dressed, her movements brisk and purposeful. Her eyes swept the room with steady focus, not a flicker of hesitation. I should've been used to her workwear by now, but I wasn't. Tight black jeans and a fitted black company shirt clung in all the right places. God, jeans were made for her body. I'd only seen her in a dress twice, at the charity gala and when we were in Pensacola.

I picked up my coffee. "You're early."

She grabbed a cup and popped two muffins in the oven. "We've got a final inspection today. House we're handing over."

Elana paused, grabbing oranges, strawberries, and other fruit. "Not sure if you'd call it a house. More like a modern-day mansion. They bought three properties and made them one. Massive place." Her eyes widened slightly as if to emphasize her last two words.

She brought the fruit bowl over right as the oven pinged. The sweet scent of warming muffins drifted through the air, mingling with the citrusy sharpness of freshly cut oranges. She added one to a plate and set it next to my bowl. Then she sat down at the island and prayed.

"No fruit for you?"

"I'm eating and running. Long day ahead. We need some groceries. I'll stop by the supermarket on my way home."

The way she said 'home' did something to me, confirmed a spark of hope I carried about us. She didn't even realize it slipped from her mouth.

I walked her to the door and kissed her cheek. Didn't trust myself with her lips. She was in a hurry, and her lips? My drug of choice. There was no such thing as a quick kiss with her. She would have been late. Once I tasted those rosy lips, I turned into an addict, craving the next hit. Restraint was safer. Better not to even start.

Back at the laptop, I slipped onto the barstool at the island and resumed working. I spent three hours digging through Jameson's digital trail. As a senior partner in a law firm with high-profile clients, you'd think he'd have better security. People hear about breaches and hacks, but they never think it'll happen to them.

I paused to order lunch, enough for dinner too. While I waited, I mulled over the data. Jameson had been siphoning funds into a shell company. Large amounts, though not the smoking gun I needed. Still, his partners would want to know. Nearly five million in the last two years, taken in small, careful increments.

Biting into my grilled chicken sandwich, I pulled out my phone. My fingers hovered. I didn't usually send threats. But Liliana needed reminding.

Want to know why I never returned your calls? Because I don't date women who sleep with married men. Stay away from Elena, or this picture of you crawling on your knees to your boss goes viral. All hopes of his political career would be over. After all, it's his wife who holds the purse strings. I doubt she'd fund the campaign of a cheating husband. She'd more likely hire a damn good divorce lawyer.

Two ticks appeared. Message delivered and read.

Finishing the sandwich and salad, I went back to work. Jameson sat on several boards, even one for a nonprofit that promoted moral ethics in society. Ha! Hypocrisy at its finest.

A few more clicks brought up a directorship in a company he held significant shares in: Nano Health Care. A quick search revealed they were a leading pharmaceutical company focused on cancer research. Their latest project: a drug to prevent pancreatic cancer in people with a specific gene that increased their risk.

Pancreatic cancer?

Interesting.

I slammed the screen shut. Jameson Wakefield didn't care about curing cancer. He cared about making sure his investment paid off.

Another puzzle piece ...

Still not quite the smoking gun. But getting close.

Forty-One

Elena

This house was an architectural marvel wrapped in glass, stone, and steel. Five acres of property, with the house itself spreading over one acre. We did the walk-through together.

A cool breeze carried the scent of freshly cut grass as we walked the perimeter, checking motion lights. The house was fully designed to run on solar power, with the electrical grid as backup. A solar-powered generator would activate first, the system only switching to the main grid if that failed. Ideally, they would never need to rely on external power at all.

With the kind of money these people spent, they could have built their own island, just like Palm Island in Dubai.

Inside, every footstep echoed against the polished marble floors. The ceilings stretched high enough to make you feel small, and sunlight poured in through walls of glass that framed the grounds like art. You needed a golf cart to get from one wing to the next.

Thank God the estate project was finally signed off.

Given the size of the house, we spent the entire day there. Mark and I had planned to go over the hospice project afterward, but that would have to wait.

Walking into my office and sinking into the chair, with the estate sign-off behind us, my mind strayed to Alejandro's discovery about Yacena. Why did she lie? She didn't have to. She could've said there'd been a recent uptick in cremations. But now I couldn't ask her anything.

The team filtered out just before closing, given that we didn't get the opportunity to grab lunch today. Mark offered to draft the final report for the contractor who hired us. The least I could do was stay and keep him company while he worked.

So ... no more questions for Yacena.

When I arranged the thank-you lunch for the hospital staff, part of the plan was to gather information by talking with Paula. But the moment Dr. Suleman appeared, something in her shifted. Her shoulders locked, jaw clenched, like she was holding something in with everything she had. She clamped down tighter than a sealed valve.

She knew something. That much was written across every tense line on her face.

Mark probably had another thirty minutes. I pulled up a search on the good doctor. The algorithms favored him; his name topped the results. He was prolific in academic journals, especially on cancer research. Photo after photo showed him presenting at conferences, always in a sharp, tailored suit, his expression calm but commanding, like he knew more than anyone else in the room. In one photo, he stood mid-gesture beside a glowing slide of cancer cells data, eyes intense and mouth slightly parted as he spoke. I clicked on a link for DaCosta Biopharma, a major pharmaceutical company.

There he was. Board of Directors. Dr. Brian Suleman.

The clock on my screen read 4:26 p.m. Maybe if I called, I could confirm whether he still sat on the board.

I skimmed the Current Research tab, groundbreaking pancreatic cancer treatment, a joint effort between the company and a private donor. Picking up the phone, I dialed the number listed on the contact page.

"Good afternoon. I've been trying to reach Dr. Suleman and saw he's listed as one of your directors. I was hoping to speak with him about his cancer research."

There was a pause before the woman replied, "Let me check." She placed me on hold.

I kept searching while I waited and stumbled on an article about his daughter being expelled from university. I wondered what that was all about.

A few minutes later, she returned. "He still serves on the board and is currently working with St. Andrews Hospital."

I dialed Alejandro, switched to speaker, and started shutting down my system. His deep voice settled something in me I hadn't even realized was stirred.

"I'm waiting on Mark," I said. "So, I did a little digging."

"Same here."

"What did you find?"

"Jameson Wakefield, Liliana's boss, is on the board of Nano Health Care. Also, a major shareholder."

"Pharmaceutical company?" I inquired.

"Big in cancer research."

I leaned forward in my chair. It had to be coincidence. But it didn't feel like one.

"My digging turned up something else," I said. "Dr. Suleman is on the board of DaCosta Biopharma."

"Give me a second." His keyboard clicked in the background. "They're competitors."

"DaCosta Biopharma and Nano Health Care?"

"Yeah. Whoever gets their drug to market first takes the lion's share. Second place could cost billions."

Mark appeared at my office door. I ended the call after reminding Alejandro I had to stop by the supermarket. Mark, ever the gentleman, walked me to my vehicle and made sure I got in safely.

The conversation played on a loop in my head. Was there a connection? No concrete link yet. Just fragments and intuition, and that hollow feeling in my gut I'd learned not to ignore.

I pressed the start button and pulled out of the parking space. Making the curve by the wall to exit, a screech of tires caught my attention. A black van tore across the lot, coming right at me. The engine snarled like a caged animal let loose. I inhaled sharply, heart hammering, and jammed the gear into reverse, hoping to avoid the collision. But the jolt of impact rattled through my spine as the truck slammed into the front right side of my vehicle, pinning me to the wall.

I screamed till my throat hurt.

The steering wheel bit into my palms, and the seatbelt dug into my ribs like a vice. The van revved again, smashing into the passenger's side. Trapped. Helpless. I couldn't open the door.

With the second impact, the glass shattered, spraying shards across my face and arms with a sting sharp as needles. The acrid tang of burning oil flooded my lungs.

So this was it. This was how I would die?

Oh God ... Dad. This would destroy him. Losing Zoë broke him. Losing me too? That would finish the job.

Then came the distant revving of an engine.

Focus, Elena.

Everything blurred. I braced for another impact.

Forty-Two

Elena

The chaotic shrieks of sirens were heard in the distance. The noise cut through my hazy mind. One sounded closer, another farther off.

Ambulance?

Fire truck?

Police?

My mind didn't allow me to distinguish between the sounds. I fought not to black out again.

The metallic tang of blood coated my tongue. A low moan escaped me. Glass crackled beneath my shifting weight. Voices blurred. The air reeked of smoke and something sharp, gasoline maybe. The world tilted sideways. Blood trickled down the side of my face. Everything hurt. I clung to the edge of consciousness, but it kept slipping through my fingers.

"Man, do you think they're alive?" a strange voice said.

"Nah… no one could survive that." Another strange voice.

Fading. Life drained from me with every breath.

Someone shouted, "Get over here!" Don't know which voice… all sounded the same now.

"Elena … Elena!" Mark's voice cracked, raw and wild. Hearing my name pulled something sharp and desperate inside me. I tried to hold on to the voice.

"It's a woman in there?"

"Yes," Mark responded.

Sorry … I'm sorry … Lord, I commit my life into …

Beep. Beep. Beep.

Harsh, artificial light flooded my vision, too white, too clinical. So … hospital.

Beep. Beep. Beep.

Air filled my lungs, sharp and cold. The mattress was rigid beneath me, the sheets tucked too tightly, trapping my legs in place. A dull ache pulsed where the IV fed into my arm. The tubing pressed against my skin. My fingers twitched against the weight of a hand.

Familiar.

Machines hummed around me. A monitor beeped, steady, high-pitched, constant. Footsteps squeaked. A distant voice paged a doctor overhead. My head throbbed. Everything came rushing back - impact, glass, screaming - and my eyes flew open. The beeping turned erratic.

"Amor... babe... Elena. The doctors are coming." Alejandro's voice was rough with emotion. His fingers threaded through mine, warm and trembling. I clung to the rough edges of his voice like a lifeline. His hand anchored me.

I turned my head, and there they were: Imani and Pastor Jonas. He held her as she cried. Imani's shoulders shook as Jonas wrapped his arms around her. She wore her grief like a second skin. It clung to every tremble in her hands and showed in the way she buried her face in Jonas's chest, as if trying to hide from a world that had broken. I wanted her to stop. To know I was okay. I wanted to call her Mom. But I never had. It always felt like a betrayal to my adoptive mother. Still, Imani had been a steady rock.

I tried to speak, to say her name, but the tube in my throat made words impossible. The plastic pressed against the back of my throat, foreign and suffocating. My mouth was dry. I gagged slightly, panicked by the inability to speak, to breathe freely.

"Zeno and your dad wanted to come, but I promised to keep them updated," Alejandro said gently.

I focused on him. He wore a wrinkled gray T-shirt, like he had picked it up off the floor and thew it on in a panic. Yet somehow it made him feel more solid, more real. In his disheveled state, he became my calm in the storm. His hair stuck out in every direction. Messy, and beautiful. He never looked more handsome.

I wanted to tell him. I wanted to say thank you. That I loved him. That I was scared.

But the tube choked the words, and whatever the nurse pushed into my IV pulled me under again, with the knowledge that someone had tried to kill me.

Forty-Three

Bishop

When Zeno Callos's name lit up my screen, an eerie chill spiked my gut. Zeno didn't make social calls. He wasn't checking to see how I was doing.

Something was wrong.

I swiped my thumb on my phone, and the second I answered, his voice came through like a whip. Words not found in Webster's Dictionary were hurled at me. He strung together curses so creatively I half expected sparks to shoot from the phone. I was pretty sure he invented some on the spot. My ear burned from the heat of it, and I had to pull the phone back. He ended the call by threatening to come for his sister if I couldn't keep her alive.

Once I pieced together what had happened, I bolted out the door. All I could hear was my pulse pounding in my ears.

I never experienced fear like that in my life. God, I didn't want to ever again.

Thank you, Jesus. She was home now after a week in the hospital. Healing, but home. I did not trust the hospitals here, so I airlifted her to Tampa. I had been stationed in her room like a soldier on duty, watching every rise and fall of her breath. God, I almost lost her. And I hadn't even told her I loved her.

Our relationship deepened in that hospital room. There were times when Imani or the nurse wasn't there, and I helped her to the bathroom, walking beside her with the IV pole and cords dragging behind. Her fingers gripped my forearm. I steadied her, every step a quiet prayer, thanking God she was alive. I undressed her because she couldn't bend down, my hands trembling as I tried to protect what dignity she had left.

I cared for Elena because I loved her. Sometimes we wonder what love is, but love is this: Being there in someone's weakest moment and not looking away. It's not about dinners and dates. It's about showing up in the ugly moments.

The rhythm of her breathing anchored me. My hand rested on hers, but my mind returned to the wreckage. I saw her vehicle, twisted metal curled like a broken ribcage. Flames hissed from the hood. Sirens screamed in the distance. They had been cutting her out when I arrived. I prayed she would survive, even though a part of me whispered that no one could walk away from something like that.

But I had called on God, in English and Spanish, for a miracle.

Hope and fury twisted together inside me as I watched them pull her out.

Now, I kissed her hand. Her eyes fluttered open.

"Didn't mean to wake you."

"You need to get some rest," she murmured, chastising me with that gentle voice.

I wouldn't rest. Not until I got my hands on the man who had done this. Him and whoever else had been behind it. I didn't know what we walked into. We didn't start this. But I was prepared to end it.

Her fingers reached up, brushing the space between my brows. "What's bothering you?"

"Thinking," I said, releasing some of the tension I carried as I exhaled.

"That chair more than likely cost a fortune. Everything in your house probably does. But I'd really love it if you'd climb into bed and hold me while I fall back asleep."

She blinked slowly, fighting the exhaustion. It would take her soon enough.

I did what she asked: Eased onto the mattress beside her and pulled her gently into my chest. Her soft hair carried its familiar peppermint scent. I nuzzled closer, breathing her in. Eventually, her breathing slowed, a warm puff of air against my collarbone, and I held her as she drifted off.

Drago and I reviewed the video footage from all three attacks: Paula, Elena's dad, and now her. Hours of surveillance, frame by frame. It was the same man every time. Of course they had used the same hitman. Less mess. Fewer loose ends.

The footage was crisp. Too crisp. We studied it together over a conference call, watching his stride, casual. His face, calm. Zeno, crazy as he was, had cameras hidden on the light poles in the parking lot. Hidden to the naked eye, but they had given us a clean shot of the guy's face before he pulled on his mask sixty seconds before he pressed the gas and accelerated to take out Elena.

Wearing a mask while waiting in a vehicle would've drawn attention. He timed it with precision. The video footage showed he had been watching her for two days.

Two days.

He picked the wrong people to mess with.

I sent Jaden to retrieve him. Jaden asked, "Dead or alive?"

Alive. I wanted him alive.

Forty-Four

Bishop

The man tied to the chair could've stepped out of a suburban catalog shoot. Clean-cut. Composed. The kind of guy who probably spent his weekends comparing cereal brands in aisle three. Early thirties, medium build, clean-shaven, freshly trimmed brown hair. His jeans hung neatly, and his plain T-shirt had probably been clean before Jaden snatched him. He had the kind of face people trusted without thinking, pleasant enough but forgettable in the way dangerous people often are. The guy next door. The one who smiled when he mowed his lawn. The last person anyone would suspect of being a professional killer.

I glanced at Jaden. "You didn't even alert me you were in Miami."

Dressed in black jeans and a gray button-down, Jaden shrugged. "Traveling south." He tilted his head toward the man. "He messed with someone you care about. That was enough to make it my priority. Plus, I wanted to be here to save you from yourself."

I instructed Jaden to use the small meeting room at the foundation. It was so out of the way, we seldom brought visitors to it. I waited until Elena drifted off to sleep before joining him. I pulled a chair and sat across from the man who tried to kill Elena. "You've been busy."

People have always described killers as having beady, soulless eyes, cold and unreadable, like glass marbles that never blink. But his eyes? They were crystal blue. A smirk sat casually on his face.

"You know, it's against the law to hold me," he said.

"Hold you?" I turned to Jaden with a raised brow and a glint in my eye. "Have you seen me touch him?"

Leaning against the wall with his feet crossed at the ankles, Jaden answered, "No clue what he's talking about."

I faced the man. "So Carl, here's the deal. You're only getting one chance."

"I suggest you let me go, and I won't press charges. I was shopping when something pricked me. Next thing I know, I'm here. You've clearly mistaken me for someone else."

Gotta admire how he kept the boy-next-door act going. He really thought we were that gullible. Jaden wheeled him into the foundation's conference room in a large crate labeled *Security Equipment*. One thing our job has taught us after years of dealing with people so hideous, who were considered to be the cesspool of earth's population, was to be resourceful.

"Carl Whitman. You're a long way from Alaska. Enjoying the warmth of Miami?"

His mouth tightened. "Listen, I told you. Let me go, and I won't go to the cops."

I shook my head. "Murder. *Attempted* murder. Breaking and entering, don't forget assault. Please, call the police. You can even use my phone."

"Wrong man."

His calmness gave him away. An innocent man would've been panicking. Would maybe even wet himself. He wouldn't be sitting there like we were discussing the weather.

"See, Carl, what gave you away was your last job." I tilted my head toward Jaden. "Play it."

Jaden turned on the sixty-inch television mounted on the conference room wall. Carl's face was paused on the screen, taken from one of the hidden cameras at the back of the parking lot. The camera directly faced the driver's seat. No side angle. Zeno was nothing if not pedantic about his family's safety.

"Press play."

The footage showed Carl pulling on a mask as he sat in a blacked-out Ford F-250 Super Duty before it roared to life and went racing towards Elena's vehicle, striking it twice, then reversing.

I balled my fist on seeing it again. Each view didn't make watching it easier, it made it worse, much worse. I could have lost Elena.

His jaw clenched.

"Nothing to say now? That same mask, with red tears under the eyes, was worn by the man who killed the nurse a few weeks ago. That wouldn't be you now, would it?"

Carl went from calm to thrashing in the chair, his face contorted with rage, veins bulging at his temple. He jerked violently against the restraints, teeth bared like a cornered animal. "Wait till I get my hands on you two ... I'll kill you both."

Jaden stepped forward and grabbed Carl's shirt. "I don't take kindly to threats. I can make you disappear in a hundred different ways."

"You never knew how to play nice."

Jaden shrugged.

After a moment, I stood up and stared at the man. "Do two things for me, and we can pretend this never happened. You leave this state and never return. Because if anything happens to Elena, or me, or anyone connected to us, with all that we've gathered, including the half-million dollars that showed up in your account around the same time as each hit, I'd be happy to bring you down to the police station. That money's more than a coincidence, I would say."

Carl blinked. "What's the second thing?"

"Who hired you?"

"I don't know."

"Wrong answer." I slammed a fist across his face. "Let's try that again. Who hired you?"

"Man, if I knew, I'd tell you." A drop of blood slid from his busted lip.

I shook my head. “You took three contracts and don’t know who hired you? Not buying it.”

“I’m telling you the truth. All my contact said was it was a woman. No name.”

A woman?

His eyes pleaded with me to believe him.

I nodded to Jaden.

He stepped forward and began untying the ropes as I opened the door. The soft creak of hinges was followed by the crisp shuffle of polished shoes on the tile. Two FBI agents walked in, suits pressed, eyes sharp.

Carl’s voice rose. “Hey! What the F...!” He wriggled under his restraints.

I held his gaze, letting the silence stretch just long enough for the truth to settle in. My pulse didn’t even flinch. He really thought he could mess with people that I cared about and then walk out of this room a free man?

As the agents moved toward him, I smiled. “I lied.”

Forty-Five

Bishop

A woman.

Everything from last year replayed in my mind. The setup at last year's fundraiser, the visit to Elena's office, the planted bug. We found it after Elena's accident, during the sweep of her office. Hidden beneath the chair where Liliana rested her bag. That alone warranted this visit.

My gaze swept over the bed. Matte black posts rose like sentinels. Sheer charcoal panels framed an emerald velvet headboard. The whole thing screamed Wicked Witch of the East more than modern-day princess. Even in sleep, her lips curled into a vicious smirk. My stomach twisted. She probably dreamed of the chaos she'd orchestrated, basking in her own deception. Rage flickered beneath my skin. How many lives had she toyed with, smiling like that?

I yanked the covers off her, and she shot upright, eyes locking on mine instantly. But when she realized it was me, she relaxed, stretching like a cat in heat.

"Elena couldn't satisfy you?"

I snatched the robe off the foot of the bed and tossed it at her. "Put that on."

She stood, making a performance out of tying the robe. Sorry, that ship sailed and sunk. Nothing she did stirred anything in me except disgust.

Once she finished tying the robe, I nodded. "Sit down."

She pulled her hair over one shoulder, batting her lashes like this was some kind of sick roleplay game.

"You can drop the act. We found the bug. Why?"

Her eyes widened. "What are you talking about?"

"Don't play dumb. I could have you arrested as an accessory to attempted murder."

She shot to her feet. "Listen to me. I planted the bug, that's all. Jameson asked me to."

"Why?"

"He's representing a client who wants to build a case against a contractor that works with Elena's company. That's why I planted the bug. We've done it before to get leads."

"What's Jameson's connection to Nano Health Care?"

"They're one of our clients. He has a directorship with the company. Why?" She crossed her arms.

"That's all?" My molars pressed tight, and heat crawled up the back of my neck.

She nodded. Too calm. Too smooth. She'd rehearsed this. The lie slid off her tongue like she'd practiced it in front of a mirror.

I shook my head. "Why are you with him? And why get involved with me? Was that just to cover up your affair?"

She bit her lip and exhaled a shaky breath, like she wasn't sure if she should be ashamed or proud. "I actually love him. The power he commands." Her voice wavered, but the glint in her eyes said she already made peace with whatever line she had crossed.

She tossed her hair back, defiant. "I'd do anything he asked. Even pretend to be in a relationship with you to keep his wife off his back."

But Carl's contact had said it was a woman. The pieces didn't fit. Was she covering for someone? Or was I missing something bigger, someone else pulling the strings?

"What about murder?"

Resting her hands on her hips, she met my stare. "I would do anything for Jameson. Anything ... except that."

Forty-Six

Elena

The rich scent of rosemary and roasted lamb curled through the air. My stomach gave a hopeful growl. Dinner couldn't come fast enough. Imani arrived with all the trimmings for dinner and promptly took over the kitchen. Pastor Jonas was in charge of dessert and would arrive soon.

I set the table, even placing a bottle of red wine in an ice bucket to chill. Alejandro selected it from his collection, said it would pair well with the lamb. I was no wine sommelier, or even that into wine in general, so I took him at his word. The label read *Sassicaia* in elegant script on textured cream paper, simple and understated, like something you'd find in a quiet Italian vineyard.

Sitting at the island, I sifted through everything Alejandro shared with me that morning. To give Imani space to work her magic, he moved to his home office. I liked knowing he wasn't far away. The steady rhythm of his presence had become something I leaned on.

He didn't need to tell me about Liliana and Carl Whitman. But I'm glad he was open and honest with me. He assured me Carl was in FBI custody and wouldn't be seeing the light of day anytime soon. Apparently, Carl was wanted for crimes in multiple states, and a few other countries. The thought that I'd been in the crosshairs of someone like that chilled me.

Alejandro wanted to know who hired Carl. He didn't think it was Liliana. According to him, she was many things but not a killer. Or at least not the kind of person who would hire one. He checked her bank account. And with sixty-five grand in her bank account, while more than the average citizen, she didn't exactly have assassin money. Unless there was a payment plan for killers.

I shook my head.

Imani walked over to the island and set down the lamb. "Penny for your thoughts?"

"Processing all that's happened these last few weeks. It's surreal. I'm just thankful to be sitting here."

She came around the island and folded me into a hug, tight, trembling, as if letting go might undo her. Her tears warmed my shoulder. "We could have lost you. *I* could have lost you."

I wrapped my arms around her shoulders. "Imani. Mom. I'm still here."

I called her Mom.

In my mind, I separated the two, so she was always Imani. My adoptive mother was Mom. But there was no doubt in my mind that Imani loved me like a mother.

"Mom. You called me Mom."

I nodded.

And her flood gates broke.

I thanked God for her. There was nothing she needed to make up for. She did the best thing when she placed me up for adoption. I found a loving family.

"Come, let's get the food on the table before Pastor Jonas joins us." She sniffled and dabbed at her eyes. Even with a hint of pink around them, she was still beautiful.

"You know that I love you," she said, giving me another hug.

The bell rang. I checked the camera and opened the door for Pastor Jonas, whose arms were full of insulated canvas totes and foil-wrapped containers.

Smiling, I asked, "Did you raid a corner bakery?"

"No bakery. This is all my mother's and housekeeper's doing."

Alejandro appeared at my side. "Well, I'll have to spend an extra thirty minutes in the gym for the rest of the week."

He took one of the bags from Pastor Jonas, who wouldn't let me take the other.

"You heard the bell? Got here quickly," I said.

He shook his head. "No, I saw when he arrived. I have a view of the lobby area."

Why would he have a view of the lobby? Maybe all the tenants could see the lobby feed, or maybe it was a perk for penthouse residents.

We gathered around the table. Pastor Jonas blessed the meal, and Alejandro gave an update about Carl Whitman, saying the investigation was ongoing. He didn't mention our little side investigation into the cremations. That would only worry Imani more. We'd all been through so much these past few months.

Imani lifted her glass. "Your birthday is two weeks away. Any plans?"

"Two weeks ago, I'd have said, 'I'm turning twenty-seven, no big deal.' But now? I want to celebrate every day God gives me." I looked at each of them. "I want everyone together. Maybe we could go to Etim?" The words came out before I could second-guess them. A celebration of life.

It was a bold request, expecting everyone to drop their plans and fly eight hours to celebrate with me.

Alejandro poured himself another glass of wine. He met my gaze over the rim of the glass, a hint of a smile tugging at his lips. "Your wish is my command."

Forty-Seven

Elena

Alejandro offered to clean up so Imani and Pastor Jonas could speak with me in private. If they thought they could fool me, they were wrong. I already knew what they wanted to talk about. Pastor Jonas loved me like he did everyone else at church, but there was no way he would keep dropping everything to accompany Imani, for example, when I was in the hospital in Tampa. I might've been pretty banged up, but because I looked like a wreck didn't mean my brain had stopped working. Actually, being forced to be still allowed me to observe things I might have missed in the past.

I led them out to the patio, where the Miami skyline stretched wide before us.

"This is some view Bishop has here," Pastor Jonas said, tilting his face to the sky.

Imani sat beside me in one of the chairs. Under the soft lighting, her hands fidgeted, fingers weaving and unweaving. I had seen her do that before, usually before singing solo at church. She could sing, sure, but when she played piano and sang? Goosebumps.

She was nervous. Her shoulders were too stiff. Her fingers were constantly twitching.

Pastor Jonas sat on my other side. They clearly thought I needed emotional support for whatever they planned to drop. He always made time for people, especially Mom. I chalked it up to his kindness. But even that started to feel personal. Honestly? I didn't mind them together. Both single. Both leaning on each other.

"I'm okay with you marrying Imani," I blurted, wanting to remove the awkwardness.

Imani leaned back while Pastor Jonas leaned forward. I weighed the possibility of them ending up together over the last week. They had history, shared values, and that quiet sort of companionship that didn't need explaining. It made sense. Sometimes they could even finish each other's sentences like an old married couple.

Pastor Jonas's brows furrowed, and Imani hands finally stilled. Had I read the situation wrong?

Pastor Jonas placed his hand on mine. "Thank you. Yes, I do want to marry Imani, and we've talked about it. I guess we were a little more obvious than we thought."

I smiled at him. "You think? The trip to visit me in Tampa was a dead giveaway."

Imani took my other hand. "You know that I love you, right?"

I nodded.

"I want to tell you a story. About when I found out I was pregnant."

Her whole passion for abstinence? It came from a cliché story. The one time she slipped, she got pregnant. Her mother found out and shipped her off to her grandmother. She never told the father. I wanted to ask why, but the look in her eyes stopped me. Her family wasn't poor, just hardworking. His family came from a completely different world. She never told her mother or grandmother who the father was. That kind of silence must've cost her.

"I moved here to Miami to be close to you," she said, squeezing my hand. Tears shimmered in her eyes. "When you turned nineteen, I found this community church online and recognized the pastor. I attended for a whole year before inviting you. When you started getting involved, Jonas asked me who you were. I told him the truth."

I turned to Pastor Jonas and said, "She did what was right. At her age, with the pressure she faced, it was the best choice. It turned out okay."

"There's no need to defend her," he replied. "I've never judged her. I've only ever loved her."

I looked between them. "What am I missing?"

Imani took my other hand again. "After spending time around you, Jonas asked me who your biological father was. Please know, I spoke to Theo before we came here tonight. After everything you've been through, I want complete honesty between us." She took a deep breath. "I told him ... he was your father."

Confused, I pulled my hand from Imani and folded my arms around myself. The air thinned, tightening in my chest. Despite the wide-open space where we sat, I needed room. I stood and walked to the balcony railing, closed my eyes, and tried to process what they just told me.

So, he's my father. I wasn't sure which emotion was supposed to come first. Relief? Anger? Confusion?

I kept circling back to Theo. He raised me. He was my dad. But what did that make Pastor Jonas now? All I knew was that everything I thought I understood about my story just shifted, and I needed time to let it settle. Time to think.

Imani came and stood beside me, "Please forgive me. He wanted to tell you. But I begged him not to. I didn't want to upset your life. He agreed to watch over you from afar."

Something in her voice tugged at me. Not guilt, not hesitation, but something softer. Familiar. Love. A mother's love.

I turned and walked back to where Pastor Jonas sat. "What made you think I was your daughter?"

"Your eyes," he said. "You have my eyes. The same vibrant, penetrating green everyone in my family has. I don't want to replace Theo. I know I can't. But I want a relationship with you, beyond being your pastor. Especially now, with me marrying your mom. I want to tell the congregation. No more secrets."

I didn't answer.

I couldn't answer ... at least not yet.

Forty-Eight

Bishop

We would land in Etim in less than fifty minutes. Elena's birthday wish to spend time with her family in Etim had been easy to plan. The last few weeks, maybe even the last few months, had been traumatic for her. Everyone on this plane wanted her to have this slice of happiness.

In these two weeks leading up to her birthday, I watched Elena swing like a pendulum from joy to confusion as she navigated having her biological parents in her life.

Right now, she sat with them and Mark playing Monopoly, of all things, which, judging by the raised voices and bursts of laughter echoing through the cabin, had gotten fiercely competitive.

Elena's brow furrowed in concentration as she moved her token with exaggerated flair, while Jonas leaned back smugly, twirling a property card between his fingers like a trophy. Imani groaned dramatically every time she landed on one of his properties, clutching her fake money to her chest as if it were real. They'd been at it for three hours, and by the looks of it, Jonas was wiping the floor with them. That should teach them not to challenge a pastor who also happened to be the son of one of the most successful hedge fund and wealth management companies in the country.

Elena was already asking for a rematch on the return trip. Who would've guessed they were all so competitive?

Imani and Jonas packed up the game while she sank into the chair next to me. "Thank God that wasn't real, or I'd have to ask you to lend me thirty grand."

"How did you end up owing thirty grand?"

"He bought everything early, all with money he borrowed from the bank. The only ones he didn't buy were Mediterranean Avenue, Baltic Avenue, and Reading Railroad. Can you believe it? Every time I pulled a card, I prayed it read 'Go to Jail'. That was one place he didn't own."

"No way," I said trying to hold back my laughter.

She shot Jonas the evil eye and raised her voice. "He never once landed on the 'Go to Jail' space. That game was rigged."

Jonas glanced over and grinned. "By the time you land back in Miami, you'll owe me close to a hundred grand."

"Mean," she muttered.

We all burst out laughing, and Elena smiled. Then she turned to me. "Thank you."

I raised a brow.

"For the last two weeks, you didn't pressure me. Didn't offer advice. You listened. Sometimes, that's all a person needs. I'm the luckiest girl alive. I have two dads. A mom who raised me. And a mother who loved me enough to let me go and then came back when I needed her the most. In prayer, I wrestled with everything. God showed me how rare and beautiful this is. To have such a blended family."

She glanced over at them, still chatting, while Mark sat reading a book. "I hope the church knows how blessed they are to have him as their pastor."

When the plane touched down, three black SUVs waited on the tarmac. As we descended the stairs, a wave of dry, sunbaked air wrapped around us, carrying the faint scent of fuel and salt. The door to the middle vehicle opened, its dark windows gleaming under the harsh light. Drago stepped out, his towering frame unmistakable, and he extended a hand to help Aimee from the vehicle. Her long, straight black hair caught the sunlight as she accepted his assistance with effortless grace.

Elena's fingers were interlaced with mine as we approached them. "Didn't expect to see you here."

"Elena, this is Aimee. And Drago, my business partner."

After introductions, Aimee walked with Elena and Imani, and we followed. I caught snippets of their conversation.

"You're going to love what Topaz got the event planners..."

Drago interrupted me by clapping a hand on my shoulder. "She's good for you. I was worried about you there for a minute. Okay, more like months." He smiled.

"Honestly, I was worried about me, too."

"Any word on who hired the guy?" Drago asked, returning to business.

My eyes stayed fixed on Elena. A twist of fear tightened in my gut. She laughed, so carefree. I couldn't stop picturing someone paying a man to kill her. In our line of work, that wasn't shocking. We never went after the innocent. Drug cartels, human traffickers, the worst of the worst. Never the innocent.

The idea of losing her before we had even begun terrified me more than I wanted to admit. And knowing that some person out there still wanted to hurt her haunted me. I increased security at the building. Whenever Elena left the house, I went with her. She hadn't returned to the office yet; she was working from home for now, but planned to go back soon.

The hit was real. His contact accepted the job through the dark web. We couldn't trace the go-between. Too many routers. Too many countries.

But the same name popped up in every message: Gran Ma. The words flashed on the encrypted screen in stark, glowing text, always at the end, like a twisted signature. No metadata. No trace. Just that name, sitting like a riddle inside every data packet we managed to intercept. It chilled me every time I saw it. Clearly a code. But a code for what?

Forty-Nine

Elena

Dad's smile came easy again. With my arm hooked through his elbow, we walked along the beach, the cool sand shifting beneath our feet with each step. A salty breeze kissed my cheeks, and the rhythmic hush of waves brushing the shore anchored me in the moment. Funny how I lived in Miami and never made time for the beach. Yet here I was, enjoying an early morning stroll with Zen's security discreetly stationed around us. As if Anson Security would ever let a single hair of any guest be harmed.

"I'm so glad I get to spend this day with you," I told Dad as we sat on the sand. The sun had fully risen, casting golden flecks across the surface of the water, while the morning air still held a refreshing coolness. The sky shimmered in soft hues of peach and lavender, painting a peaceful start to the day. "So much happened in the last few months, but having this time together means the world to me."

He wrapped his arm around my shoulder and smiled. "I'm glad you took my advice. Do you think liking Bishop makes you love God any less?"

I smiled. "I'm happy I saw past his playboy ways and got to know him." I glanced at Dad. "I love him. I haven't said it to him yet."

"What are you waiting for? Christmas?"

He nudged me to share my feelings, but I'd already planned to tell Alejandro tonight. I was ready to fully embrace this relationship. There was no doubt in my mind that he loved me. The way he watched over me. Stayed with me. Changed my hospital sleepwear without ever, even once, looking repulsed by the tubes or the mess. If anything, what we had only deepened since then.

I rested my head on Dad's shoulder. "There's so much to thank you for. Including giving Imani and Pastor Jonas your blessing to speak with me."

He gave my shoulder a gentle squeeze. "You adapted well to living with us. Even though you never said it out loud, I saw how hard you tried not to disappoint us. As much as it came from love and appreciation, part of it was rooted in fear." He smiled. "Letting Imani into your life boosted your self-confidence. What kind of father would I have been if I'd kept you from knowing your biological parents? You deserve to know you're truly loved."

We remained seated until I spotted the hostess walking toward us for the next birthday activity. The first was strolling the beach with Dad, and honestly, if that had been all, I would've been completely content.

Standing and extending my hand to him to help him up, I said, "They've found us."

"If you were trying to hide, sitting in the middle of the beach with a security team was a poor attempt at blending in."

I bumped him playfully. "Whose side are you on?"

"Always yours. Always."

When we walked into the private room, the warm aroma of baked breads blended with a medley of other mouthwatering flavors. Everyone stood and sang happy birthday. Aimee greeted me with a tight hug, and Drago raised a mimosa in a mock toast. Dad's laugh rumbled from across the room, deep and full of life. My blended family was here. New friends like Drago and Aimee. A couple I met briefly yesterday, Jaden and his wife Tanisha.

Breakfast was a buffet set up in a cozy banquet space with a terrace that overlooked the ocean. Dad stood. "I want to thank all of you for being here," he announced. "These past few months have been rough, but we got through them together. Jonas, you're the best gift I could give my daughter. Ellie, know you don't ever have to worry about making me jealous by loving Jonas, because I know you love me." Taking the champagne that was served on the table, he raised a toast.

Jonas stood and blessed the meal, and afterwards, I led the way to the buffet. As the morning went on, Topaz and Shae Anson came by in person to check that everything was to my satisfaction.

Topaz presented me with a gift followed by a quick hug. "It's a gift certificate for a spa day for two at any of the Anson properties. No expiration date. Any friend of Drago and Aimee is a friend of ours."

I thanked them and invited them to stay and spend a few minutes with us before returning to work, which they accepted happily.

The gala. Topaz Anson and Aimee Patel. The fifty-thousand-dollar dress.

Alejandro leaned into me, "I see a look on your face."

"I just remembered something from the gala."

He raised a brow.

"At the gala, an Aimee Patel gown that was worn by Topaz Anson went for fifty thousand dollars. I couldn't figure out why back then." I wagged my finger at him. "Google holds all the answers. Seems you have some well-connected friends."

He laughed and sipped his champagne.

Zen and Imani left as soon as breakfast ended. He wanted to return home to oversee the preparations for the birthday dinner he was hosting. I was certain some of these same people would be in attendance.

It appeared that Alejandro's friend and business partner, Drago, and Zen moved in the circle of the "who's who of Etim."

After breakfast, Alejandro and I strolled along the boardwalk that stretched into the ocean. Schools of fish swam beneath us, darting playfully through the clear water. The sunlight shimmered off their scales, and the gentle murmur of waves brushing against the wooden supports of the boardwalk added a tranquil soundtrack to the moment.

At the end of the boardwalk, there was a railing where we could lean and look out over the ocean. Gentle waves rolled toward the shore in rhythmic swells, the deep blue water stretching to the horizon like a velvet ribbon. Sunlight danced across the surface, making it sparkle as if scattered with diamonds. Miles and miles of endless blue.

"Gorgeous," I whispered.

"Correct. Gorgeous." His stare pressed into my skin, heat rising in my cheeks.

"You haven't even looked."

"I'm looking."

I shook my head at him.

He stepped closer, closing the distance between us. "Elena Callos ... I didn't go looking for you, but I'm glad I found you. And now that I have, I'm never letting you go. I love you. Don't know when it happened."

My breath caught. I never thought I'd hear those words, at least not meant for me. Not like this. Surrounded by sea and sky, everything in me cracked wide open. It wasn't just that he loved me. I loved him back, fully, wildly, with my whole heart.

I took his hand, pressed our intertwined fingers against my chest. "I love you too, Alejandro Bishop."

He stepped forward and kissed me, my arms winding around his neck. His lips met mine in a kiss that was tender, sure, and everything in between. It wasn't rushed. It was reverent. As if he was memorizing the feel of me, and I, him. When he finally pulled back, he reached into his pocket.

"I have something for you." He pulled out a small box.

My heart raced. We'd just said we loved each other, but—

"Don't keel over on me," he laughed at my widened eyes. "It's not an engagement ring."

Inside the box was a stunning pair of emerald studs, their rich green depth catching the morning light and flickering like a tiny flame. The gems shimmered with warmth, reminding me of the color of my eyes.

"I want you to wear these and never take them off."

"They're gorgeous, but—"

"Take them." He smiled, tracing a finger, along my jawline. "But they aren't for show. One earring has a tracker, the other a microphone. And this little device ..." He handed me something that looked like a car fob. "Keep it in your pocket at all times. Press here to activate, and I can hear anything in your vicinity. It's connected to my watch."

"I feel like James Bond being decked out for his next mission. You really know how to woo a girl with gifts," I teased.

He tilted my chin up and brushed a kiss over my lips. "When I ask you to marry me, not if but when, I'll kneel. Not on one knee. On both."

Fifty

Bishop

The others filed into the conference room for our midweek meeting. Five cases were on the list requesting assistance, though more could be added if they came in after the report was submitted. Danielle was set to return to the foundation in two weeks. She'd agreed to a hybrid schedule for the first year so she could spend more time with her daughter.

Elena returned to work one week after we got back from Etim. Zeno stationed a bodyguard outside her door, a broad-shouldered man with a buzz cut and a stare that could freeze lava, and two more at the building's entrance, both built like linebackers and carrying the same no-nonsense edge. They didn't just stand there; they scanned every movement like predators on high alert. All former military, trained to kill or be killed. Even for me who had worked in the field, these guys were terrifying. Elena tolerated it because it helped everyone around her feel safer. I drove her to and from work with the guards tailing us. I arranged for them to stay in the penthouse two floors down.

None of us would rest until we found out who placed the hit on her. I scanned my finger and punched in the passcode to wake up my tablet. "Let's get started."

All five cases were straightforward, families with no insurance seeking financial help to cover medical expenses. One of the patients recently celebrated their first birthday. My chest tightened as I thought of Danielle cradling her newborn. That image alone made it impossible to say no. I rubbed the back of my neck, the weight of helplessness pressing down hard. "Let the family know we'll cover all medical and related costs," I said, my voice low. It was the least we could do, even if it never felt like enough. God, I wished we could actually find a cure for this disease.

"This might be the shortest meeting ever," I said as we wrapped up the list. "Any more requests?" I turned to Camila.

"Two," she replied. "The first is a little different, but I want us to consider it." She explained the situation. A daughter wanted to take three months off work to be with her dying mother. Doctors had given the mother two months. Though the leave was approved, the daughter couldn't afford to be without a paycheck. She was asking for living expenses to be covered.

The charity wasn't set up to handle expenses like that. "Would our auditors allow an exception?"

"I doubt it," she mumbled.

"Send me the information. I'll handle it outside the foundation."

"You'll cover the cost?"

"Send me the information."

A smile broke out across her face. "You're not Scrooge after all."

My brows drew together. "Scrooge?"

She breezed past it. "The next case. A family needs legal representation. It's identical to what brought Elena to us. Same hospital. The mother came into the office." Her chest rose and fell. "This one's worse. She was sick for three days and couldn't get to the hospital. When she finally arrived, they claimed they tried to contact her, but the body was already cremated."

"What?" I snapped.

Still watching me, she added, "They told her she could collect the ashes—"

Leaning forward and resting my hand on the conference room table, I said, "Let me guess. From Everlight Funeral Services."

Her eyes narrowed. "How did you—?"

My jaw clenched as fury bubbled beneath the surface. I stood, grabbing my tablet with fingers that trembled just enough to betray the restraint I was barely holding on to. "Lucky guess."

It was time to pay Nathan Carmichael a visit. There was no way he could be CEO of the hospital and not know what was going on. I called Jaden and asked him to check Nathan's accounts for anything suspicious. I kicked myself. I let our friendship cloud my judgment. By the time I pulled into St. Andrew's Hospital, Jaden had confirmed there were no odd financial movements. Just salary and regular household deductions. Not even a bar tab. According to Jaden, his life revolved around work and family.

I didn't want to believe Nathan was turning a blind eye to this. Memories of us partying during our college days flooded my mind. A knot tightened in my gut.

When I walked into his office, he stood and shoved his hands into his pockets. "If your jaw gets any tighter, it might fracture."

I didn't laugh.

He gulped. Sitting, he added, "Okay, that look tells me this isn't a social visit."

"Ever heard of Everlight Funeral Services?"

"Should I have?"

I pulled up the files I'd compiled, showing him the link between recent cremations at both hospitals and young women with pancreatic cancer.

"Man ... This can't be happening. There has to be an explanation."

"Something's going on, and your hospital's involved. You better start asking questions before you end up on the front page."

I stood. "I like you, Nathan. But friend or not, if you're involved in this, I won't hesitate to put you behind bars ... at best."

Fifty-One

Elena

I turned off the oven. Mom and Pastor Jonas – Dad – were coming over for dinner.

Mom and Dad. Except I hadn't called him that. Not since the revelation. I hadn't called him anything, really. In my head, the two aspects of him started to blend: Pastor and Dad. When I wanted to speak with him, I ensured that I was in a position where I didn't need to call his name.

Very mature of me.

I shook my head and reached for the wine glasses.

"Something smells amazing," Alejandro whispered against my ear. "Let me get those for you."

I stayed pressed against the counter as he reached around me and took down the four glasses, resting them gently beside me. He didn't move away. Instead, he placed soft kisses down my neck.

"For the record, the food smells good ... but that wasn't what I meant."

So far, we'd only kissed, nothing more. He respected my need to take things slow. Still, with his body pressed against mine and his mouth against my neck, warmth bloomed in my chest and spread lower, tugging at something deep inside me. I told myself to breathe and repeated the word *slow* in my mind like it was on a loop. But every inch of my traitorous body wanted to lean in, to feel more. My fingers curled slightly against the counter, grasping for control even as my body betrayed me with a shiver of anticipation. When he brushed my hair aside, kissed my neck, then gently bit, sucked, and licked the same spot, my eyes fluttered shut. I melted into him, and a soft moan escaped.

I could feel him smile slightly, still kissing the curve of my neck. His arousal pressed into me, undeniably.

My eyes flew open. "I can feel your—"

He turned me around and tilted my face up to his. "I can control myself. But that's my body's natural response to you."

"I know you can," I whispered.

His shirt gaped slightly at the collar, revealing his neck. I leaned in, tongue darting out hesitantly. He inhaled sharply. The low hiss that escaped him spurred me on.

"You little minx," he teased. "You better stop before your parents think I'm corrupting their daughter."

I fluttered my lashes at him. "But you are."

He laughed. "Let me get the wine. How about we eat by the pool?"

It had been a hectic week. Then came the news on Wednesday about another family who suffered the same fate we did with Zoë. We visited them yesterday. Alejandro agreed to take on their case to sue the hospital. In their daughter's case, there wasn't even paperwork. Camila sent a letter to the hospital, and this morning, Nathan called. He'd managed to get a meeting with the board after emailing them his preliminary findings.

The doorbell chimed and Alejandro let my parents in.

Imani came into the kitchen and hugged me. She glanced around with wide eyes. "Let me help with the food. Bishop said we're eating by the pool, and I'd love to see more of this fantastic house."

I walked over to Pastor Jonas—no, Dad—and wrapped my arms around him. He hugged me back, his green eyes searching mine.

"How are you doing?"

Laughing, I said, "My life is completely different than it was four months ago, that's for sure."

"That doesn't answer the question. How are you really doing?"

"I'm... surprisingly good." Everything that happened still shook me, but I couldn't help feeling grateful for the good it brought. Alejandro. My biological parents. And the chance not to bury my head in the sand, to stand up for Zoë, and to keep working at uncovering the truth.

Alejandro led the way toward the pool area, and we followed close behind. The sound of gently circulating water echoed in the open space, calm and serene. Potted palms and lush greenery lined the perimeter, giving it a resort-like feel despite being indoors. On one side, sleek lounge chairs invited relaxation, and on the other, a rectangular table set for four waited for our arrival. Imani had helped lay out the food earlier. Nothing fancy, but it was fitting for a Friday night. Sautéed chicken with vegetables, baked sweet potatoes, and fried plantains.

Pastor Jonas...Dad... prayed, and we spent time catching up. Imani and Pastor Jonas said they planned to announce their engagement to the church. He also wanted to share the truth about us. It was a risk; he could lose members. Even though it had been over twenty-seven years and he had been a teenager at the time, people would still judge. But he didn't want to keep me a secret.

My heart warmed. They were willing to wait until I was ready to tell the congregation, but he wanted to tell his family now. Something in me cracked open. I hadn't realized how much I needed to hear that, how much I'd feared being hidden or tucked away like a mistake.

Alejandro's hand settled on mine. I smiled at him, at Pastor Jonas. "Remember what you asked me a moment ago?"

He nodded.

"A lot is changing. But I welcome it," I said softly.

We shifted to lighter topics like church picnic plans and the summer internship program. Alejandro joined in, offering suggestions for picnic locations. I loved that he didn't sit back when the topic switched to church.

Then the bell chimed. All conversation paused. I turned instinctively to Alejandro. Our eyes locked, and I raised a brow. "Expecting someone?"

Fifty-Two

Bishop

To get to my door and press the bell, the person had to be on my preapproved visitors list. No way would the concierge let anyone up otherwise.

The camera feed lit up on my phone. I blinked once, then again, slower the second time. A crease formed between my brows as my jaw shifted. "What's he doing here?"

I stood up from the table. "Excuse me." I met Elena's eyes. "It's Nathan."

"Why don't we all move inside for coffee and dessert?" Imani asked, rising to her feet and picking up her plate.

"Leave them. Elena and I will tidy up later. Coffee sounds good. Let me go greet Nathan."

The others went to the kitchen while I pressed the door open for Nathan. A deep, furious red colored his face, like he had been holding his breath too long. His jaw clenched. His eyes weren't just wide, they were wild. Bloodshot. Almost shaking in their sockets.

He stood in front of me. "I called a meeting with the oncology unit about Camila's letter. She intends to bring legal action against the hospital on behalf of the family. Two hours later, the chairman of the board emailed me. I was fired." He ran a hand through his hair.

"They offered me a thirty-million-dollar separation package. Ten more than was in my contract. Never saw a decision made so fast in that hospital yet. That tells me they're hiding something. So, I figured I had nothing to lose. I decided to expose them before they made me the scapegoat."

Elena walked toward us. "Hi, Nathan. Want to join us for some coffee?"

He turned to her. "Maybe something a little stronger than coffee."

As we walked toward the kitchen, I asked, "What do you mean, you decided to expose them?"

He glanced at his watch. "I'll show you in about fifteen minutes."

I poured him a whiskey on the rocks. Imani and Elena placed coffee and apple pie on the counter while Pastor Jonas pulled the ice cream from the freezer.

And in that moment, I realized ... my house had turned into a home. For years, it stood quiet, pristine but hollow. It now pulsed with life. With purpose. Maybe this is what I'd been missing.

Elena.

Laughter.

Noise.

Talking.

Even with a distraught, jobless friend in the mix.

Nathan kept peeking at his watch. At nine o'clock, he turned on the television to a local news channel. Ten minutes in, he appeared on screen beside the same woman who'd came to the foundation about her daughter being cremated without the family's permission.

We all moved into the living room, the hum of the TV growing louder as we settled onto the couches. The scent of cinnamon from the pie lingered in the air. Elena's hand hovered near her mouth. Pastor Jonas leaned forward, elbows on his knees. Nathan sat upright, shoulders squared, his eyes locked on the screen like he couldn't believe the words were his. No one spoke. The tension coiled, waiting for whatever came next.

Nathan told the reporter he'd been fired after raising concerns about a family's daughter being cremated without their consent. He mentioned other cases that seemed suspicious and said authorities should investigate.

I faced him. "You know they probably won't pay you a cent now."

He didn't even blink. "Bishop, this happened on my watch. After everything I did for these families, I let them down. Money be damned."

In that moment, I couldn't have been prouder of my friend.

Elena and I still needed to fill her parents in on what was unfolding and how we were both involved.

But that news piece wasn't just a spanner in somebody's work. Nathan threw an entire wrecking ball, and I could bet that somebody, somewhere, was not going to take this sitting down. Not with billions of dollars on the line.

Fifty-Three

Elena

Everyone had finally gone. With the kitchen tidied, we slid down onto the living room floor, our backs resting against the sofa. The room was dim, with a soft, silver glow filtering through the curtains of the open windows. Alejandro flicked through the channels.

I rested my head on his shoulder. "With so many eyes on this now, someone should uncover what's really going on."

He wrapped his arm around me, pulling me into his embrace. Heat radiated off his body, sinking into my skin and loosening the tension in my shoulders. I leaned closer, drawn to the comfort of his steady breathing, my chest rising in sync with his as a sense of calm wrapped around me. He kissed the top of my head.

"I don't know. All Nathan might have done was rattle the nest." He stroked my arm.

I tilted my head back. The space between his brows creased. "Are you worried?" I climbed onto his lap and rested my head against his chest.

"Worried? Yes. Neither of the scenarios running through my head is good."

"Tell me."

"If the spotlight gets too bright," Alejandro said, his voice low, "the mastermind might go quiet, start covering their tracks. Hide the evidence, bury the links. Or panic and strike again."

He didn't say it aloud, but I knew what he meant. The two possible targets were Nathan or me. And Nathan was too public to be hit right now.

That only left me.

And I hated the way my skin prickled with the thought. The last time, I landed in the hospital. As much as I loved Jesus, I wasn't ready to meet Him yet. I wanted to get married. Strange, when that idea wasn't even on the same planet as me five months ago. Maybe I even wanted to start a family someday. There was so much I wanted to do.

Nope. Not ready to meet my Maker yet.

"Elena, I need you to be extra careful. I'm not trying to make you a prisoner. But for the next few weeks, the security detail stays with you, even if you're only heading to the water fountain on the next floor."

"No arguments here," I said, lifting my face to his.

He brushed a kiss over my lips. "To be safe, let's limit outings to work and home. Nothing more." His arms tightened around me, as if shielding me from a danger only he could sense.

Fifty-Four

Elena

Running my hand down my pants pocket, I pressed the tiny remote. "Alejandro ... can you hear me? Still feels unfair that your birthday gift lets you eavesdrop, but I can't respond. I guess that's why they call it a listening device."

My cell vibrated.

> **Ms. Callos, glad to know you've arrived at work. Seems you're bored. Want me to give you a reason to play hooky?**

"Mr. Bishop," I murmured, smiling, "maybe you're the one who needs rescuing. Are you sitting there waiting to hear me talk to you?"

It comes with the watch. Which, by the way, I never take off. Missing me? I can skip this meeting. We could both play hooky.

"With Mark off on his family reunion cruise? Not happening. I'm holding down the fort. Sophie's coming. Later."

Sophie burst into the office and placed an order for two laptops and large-screen monitors on my desk for me to review. As I worked through the specs, she chatted more than usual. Enough to make me pause.

"Sophie, is something on your mind?"

Her brown eyes widened, flicking to the side before meeting mine again. She shook her head quickly, fingers worrying the edge of the folder in her hands.

I returned to the documents. Whatever it was, I guessed she didn't want to talk about it.

She shifted from foot to foot. All that movement nearly made me dizzy. "Sophie, sit down. There is no hopscotch in here."

She opened her mouth, closed it, then blurted, "I know we don't have a fraternizing policy, but I asked Mark out." She blinked like she was trying to set a world record. "Since then, we've been hanging out. Nothing serious. But I like him."

My pen froze mid-signature. I always suspected Mark had cared for Zoë. They claimed to be friends, nothing more. But he deserved happiness.

"Thanks for telling me," I said.

"I didn't want it to be awkward or a surprise if you saw us out."

I nodded. Seeing anyone out wasn't likely. My life was work and home. Sundays were the only exception, when I taught Sunday School. I wasn't about to miss my class, especially now that the internship program was in its second week.

I handed Sophie the documents. She left.

Smooth jazz drifted through the room, a mellow saxophone solo lightening my workspace. It didn't relax me entirely, but it kept the silence from swallowing me whole as I tackled the next batch of emails. Admin work wasn't my favorite, but with Dad off to some Caribbean country with Zen to buy a plantation, yes, a plantation only God knows what he planned to do with, I inherited the pile of emails.

The door opened. Imani stepped in, her sleek bob tucked behind her ears and a soft smile playing on her lips. She carried a bag in one hand and moved with the graceful ease of someone who knew she was welcome.

"You're a sight for sore eyes," I said.

She placed the bag on the desk. "That's 'So What' by Miles Davis."

The scent of smoked ham teased my nose as she leaned in and kissed my cheek, her warmth settling around me with the quiet calm only she carried. Her eyes sparkled with affection, and for a heartbeat, my shoulders dropped, only then realizing how tight they'd been.

Trust her to recognize the song. I could picture her on *Jeopardy!*: Music for 500, Alex.

"The mountain has come to Muhammed," she teased, settling into the chair opposite.

"Bishop has you on lockdown, but I figured we could still have lunch here. I even brought lunch for your security." She bowed her head to pray, then tore into her sandwich. "Can't have them collapsing while they're supposed to be protecting you."

Between bites, she asked, "So, have you heard anything?"

I set down my sandwich. "It's been quiet the last few days. Maybe they've gone into hiding."

"Let's hope the FBI or someone catches them soon."

That hope topped my prayer list.

She finished her sandwich. "Bishop came to church. First time you ever brought a guy."

"First, I'm staying with him. Second, there was no way he was letting security drive me when he was home to do it. It just made sense for him to stay."

"I'm glad he came," she chuckled at my defensiveness. "You two look good together."

"Don't go planning a wedding yet. I'm still adjusting to being in a relationship. I skipped the training wheels and jumped straight onto a motorcycle."

"Do you love him?"

Heat rushed to my face as I thought about him. "More than I ever thought possible."

"You deserve it. You look out for everyone. It's time to look out for yourself."

She kissed my cheek, cleaned up our lunch mess, and left.

Two project proposals waited for me. I requested an extension. Mark's input was essential, and I wouldn't interrupt his vacation.

My phone buzzed. My heart gave a small jump, I already knew it was him. Alejandro. The thought of seeing his name lit something warm in my chest.

On my way to pick you up.

I spent the entire day at my desk. My back needed a break. I could pack up and wait in the lobby.

Leaning forward, I reached out to shut down the computer. An email flashed into my inbox. I considered leaving it for tomorrow, but it would only get lost in the pile by morning. I clicked it open.

My gut twisted.

Not what I needed. Not with a stretched-thin team and mounting deadlines.

Alejandro would not be pleased.

Not at all.

Fifty-Five

Bishop

We arrived in Pensacola this morning. I dropped Elena at the hotel with one member of the security team. She mentioned a final meeting before breaking ground on the hospice project. Definitely work related. But I wanted us back on the plane to Miami by tomorrow morning. We'd been limiting our movements these past few days, and this meeting was last minute. Given the sudden nature of this trip, it was the perfect opportunity to plan a romantic dinner by the water.

With only one security team member present, I told her to keep the fob in her pocket and press it at the top of every hour. Just for my peace of mind. I'd already spoken to Zeno about the trip; he gave the other two team members the weekend off. If anything happened to Elena, Zeno would want to skin me alive. He'd have to wait in line because I would be first.

Dinner was booked, so I brought my laptop out to the patio where the salty breeze tangled through my hair and the golden light shimmered across the ocean's surface. The rhythmic hush of waves rolling onto shore blended with the distant cries of seagulls, creating a tranquil backdrop for work. Why didn't I come here more often? I'd be thirty-nine in a few months. Maybe penthouse living wasn't the best way to raise a family.

Family.

The word landed with a thud in my chest. A vision flashed in my head – Elena barefoot on this very patio, laughter in her throat, a toddler clinging to her leg. My pulse stuttered. Where did that come from?

Had my mind really gone there?

Elena and I hadn't even discussed having kids. It wasn't on my radar, not until sixty seconds ago.

The tension in my shoulders eased without permission, like the place itself exhaled through me. My muscles loosened, my eyelids heavy. The constant coil of alertness unwound, and for a moment, I let it.

The ocean.

The breeze.

The swaying leaves.

But the peace didn't last long. My mind drifted to Nathan. I still hadn't figured out why the board moved so quickly to terminate Nathan's contract and hand him a golden handshake, hoping he'd go quietly. He didn't.

Something didn't sit right.

Snippets from the meeting echoed through my watch. *The land had been cleared and was ready for us to start work on the foundation next week.*

I searched the public records again. St. Andrews Hospital: Sixty percent owned by a teaching university, the remaining forty percent by a private company. But that company wasn't listed. Instead, it pointed to a shell corporation tucked away offshore. My gut twisted. Someone was hiding something. And not just anyone. This level of secrecy didn't happen by accident.

Tracking the owners of that shell company would take hours. Elena checked in again; they were at lunch.

Two hours later, I found what I needed. Nano Health Care owned it outright.

I stood, yanked off my shirt, and dove into the water. Laps helped me think. Why would they go to such lengths to hide their ownership?

Unless they didn't want anyone to know. Unless this was a test ground. For patients. Some willing, some not.

My chest tightened. A jolt of adrenaline surged through me as the pieces snapped into place like a trap springing shut. I froze, heart hammering, my skin prickling with the sudden clarity of what this could mean.

Dragging myself out of the water, I overheard someone asking when the meeting would wrap up. They said less than two hours, and afterwards, they would go to the groundbreaking to take pictures.

That gave me time.

Time to dig deeper.

Who owned Nano Health Care? Why the secrecy?

"Why don't you let the guy from outside have a drink with us?" someone asked as the conversation filtered through my watch.

Elena answered, *"No alcohol. But he'll take coffee."*

Cheers erupted. A voice launched into a speech, but I barely registered the words. Something about extending healthcare from cradle to grave, a commitment to quality care.

The drone of corporate practiced reassurance vibrated through my watch, the kind meant to be nothing more than a PR piece. Elena checked in as promised. Safe.I focused on the laptop screen, fingers tapping anxiously against the table.

I pushed the corporate fluff out of my mind.

Then the screen blinked.

A name flashed across it, and everything stopped.

My breath caught. My chest locked up as if someone had slammed a fist into it. The codename. Gran Ma. It all made horrifying sense now.

I glanced at my watch. Ten past the hour. Elena hadn't checked in.

They were supposed to be on a site visit, but the tracker hadn't budged. Same spot. Too long.

I called her but it cut straight to voicemail. *Voicemail.* That meant her phone was turned off. She wouldn't have turned off her phone. Not with everything going on.

Dread crawled up my spine. I threw on a shirt, bolted to the vehicle, and called her bodyguard. No answer.

My soul screamed. Blood pounded in my ears. The world narrowed to a tunnel of noise and panic. My hands trembled as I gripped the wheel, lungs constricting with every heartbeat.

They had her.

I was going to get her back, and I'd burn everything in my path to do so.

Fifty-Six

Elena

Why did my head feel so heavy? Did I faint?

My limbs refused to move. Thoughts slipped like water through cupped hands. My head swam. The skin on my hand itched. I blinked. A needle. A needle... prepped for an IV. Definitely not a dream.

Nausea pressed at the back of my throat. My mouth, dry and thick, might as well have been stuffed with cotton. My lips wouldn't shape words.

My eyes adjusted to the dim light, but everything blurred around the edges.

This wasn't a hospital. No beeping monitors. No sterile chill. The sheets were soft. Too soft for a hospital.

A tall lamp stood in the corner beside a plush chair angled toward the window. Books stacked neatly nearby. A room designed for comfort. Something about it twisted my stomach.

Lavender hung in the air, pleasant at first, but a sterile edge crept beneath it. Like perfume carefully hiding something... sinister. Yes, sinister. The needle in my hand gave it away. I definitely wasn't here for relaxation.

Sunlight filtered through gauzy curtains, golden and soft. But the light didn't warm me. Distant. Unreachable.

Alejandro.

He had to be worried sick. Was he looking for me? Had someone told him? What if no one even knew I was missing?

My stomach knotted tighter.

Lamp. Chair. Flat-screen TV. All too deliberate. Like a set.

Like... a hotel room.

This was a hotel room.

Panic scratched at my chest. I needed to move my hand. Hit the button.

Come on. Move.

Every drop of energy funneled into my right hand. It trembled as I dragged it across the bed, every inch a battle. My fingers brushed the fabric of my pants. Fumbled. Slid. Found the shape.

Thank you, Jesus.

Teeth clenched, I pressed the button. My voice cracked through my raw throat.

"H'llooo ..."

Slurred. Drawn-out. Barely a whisper. But it had to be enough.

The door creaked open a few minutes later. I prayed my voice hadn't summoned the devil.

A woman stepped inside. Familiar, almost. I squinted, heart stuttering. Recognition remained out of reach, like a name or face I couldn't place. Cream slacks. Emerald blouse. Silk, not satin. Her posture screamed wealth and control. Late fifties. Flawless makeup. Hair sculpted into place.

"You're finally up," she said flatly. "Obviously a lightweight. That drug should've cleared out thirty minutes ago. I hate delays."

Her heels didn't make a sound. The floor had to be carpeted... unless she floated in, and she definitely wasn't a ghost. She stood there, in living color. But who was she?

I'd seen her face somewhere before ...

Hospital?

Work?

Television? No.

Newspaper.

Yes. The newspaper! Social pages? Business feature? The name danced out of reach.

"Yooou ... wh-whooo ... arrrre—"

My voice cracked. Lips too numb to work properly.

She reached down and tucked a loose strand of hair behind my ear, like I was a child. Like she cared about me.

"You want to know who I am?"

I blinked.

Her smile stayed soft. Practiced. Nothing behind it.

"Call me Grandma."

She leaned in closer, her breath warm against my skin. "You see, dear, I've been waiting."

A chill slid down my spine. Blood drained from my face. The puzzle piece refused to fit. Somehow, she was the queen of whatever plan had been orchestrated. The one moving the pieces around the board.

My tongue was like a lump of hardened clay in my mouth.

She pulled a chair close with effortless grace. Sat like she had nowhere else to be.

"We needed for the first drug to wear off. Now the good doctor can give you the other one. The two can't mix, otherwise they will show up in your blood work. This next one will put you to sleep ... for a very long time."

Her smile wasn't evil.

It was polished. Refined. The kind of smile that graced ribbon cuttings and charity galas. The kind that fooled you, until it didn't.

Fifty-Seven

Elena

I remembered her.

The newspaper.

The same one that reported Paula's murder. How ironic. She made the front page, while Paula's story barely filled a column on the back. The article featured Jameson Wakefield, her husband, announcing his possible Senate run. In the photo, she stared straight ahead, eyes strained, her smile taut as wire, stretched so tight it was ready to snap. Even now, her face held more ease than in that image.

Should I let her know I'd figured out who she was? Or would that put my life in even more danger? My heart thudded under the weight of the risk. If I spoke too soon, she might silence me for good. But staying quiet might mean Alejandro couldn't expose her.

Helplessness clawed at me, my mind racing while my body refused to respond. If I could just get out her name. Or get her to talk. Even if Alejandro couldn't reach me in time, maybe he could still reveal everything, assuming my one feeble attempt to hit the button worked. God, I pray he could hear.

My head twitched toward the needle.

She uncrossed and recrossed her legs. "One of Dr. Suleman's nurses placed the needle in your hand. He should be along soon to hook up the drip. The IV stand is over there. Oh ... dear, you still can't turn your head." She laughed, as if she was at a tea party and not discussing murder. "He said there's still a risk of it showing up in your system if he injected it directly into you. Can't leave any traces now. Not with what we have planned."

I needed to know why. Why was she doing this? None of it made sense. Was it about power? Money? Revenge?

My mind scrambled for connections, trying to thread together the fragments I gathered so far. But nothing fit neatly. There were the cremations, the offshore accounts. Then the hitman and the wired money. Liliana and the bug she planted in my office. But the more I thought about it, the more tangled it became. People didn't do things like this, not unless they were truly desperate. Or terrifyingly cold?

"Why?" I croaked, the word barely scraping past my throat.

She leaned forward. "You want to know why? Why you're here? That should be obvious."

My gaze locked on her face.

My tongue pushed forward, sluggish and dry, grazing my lips. Thirst clawed at my throat. But I refused to ask the woman who clearly drugged me for water.

She glanced at her watch. "Dr. Suleman should be here shortly." Then she stood and paced the room, either burning nervous energy or trying to calm herself.

When she returned to the chair, she smoothed her hair, though not a single strand was out of place. "I don't know what's keeping him. He should be back from the groundbreaking ceremony for the hospice by now."

She tapped a finger against her jaw. "You thought your little company won that project? I kicked the other company off, hoping the work would distract you from asking questions about the cremations. All while keeping an eye on you."

A sharp pulse of dread thudded behind my eyes. She gave us the project to keep me occupied. If that was the case, the company that lost the contract would have sued. But for a woman who paid to have people killed, legal fees were nothing more than pocket change.

She shook her head. "But you were like a ravenous dog who thought it found the last bone on earth. Nothing could pry it from your mouth."

She stared directly at me. Her eyes cold.... calm...calculated!

"I guess if my sister had been killed, I would be like that too. Not killed ... no, she was part of a trial that went wrong."

Trial...Went wrong?

"You see, they were all part of a trial. When we find patients with a specific type of pancreatic cancer, they're often referred to either St. Andrews or Southshore Memorial. Those hospitals are known for developing treatments for that type of cancer."

My pulse pounded louder.

"We're close. But we need another year to perfect the medication."

My heart pounded. They killed my sister. My chest caved in under the weight of the words. My brain couldn't catch up. A scream built inside me, desperate to claw its way out, but I laid still with my memories of Zoë, as a salty tear burned its way down my cheek, tracing the edge of my grief. Images of Zoë, laughing, dancing in the kitchen, hugging me tight, flashed behind my eyes. She trusted the system. She trusted me. And I failed her. I encouraged her to take part in the trial.

Me... I did that...

"Don't cry. She was going to die anyway. Maybe not as soon, but the medication had to be tested."

My stomach twisted.

"Moonney?"

She stood again and paced. "No, this was not about money." She paused. A quiet smile tugged at her mouth, reaching her eyes this time. "My granddaughter. She's thirteen, all braces and sparkles, and she still thinks I hang the moon. Believes I can make anything better. And I will. I *have to.*" Her voice softened. "A routine screening showed she carries the gene. A fifty percent chance of pancreatic cancer before she's even thirty. You think I could sit back and hope for the best?"

She paused and sat.

"You loved your sister. My granddaughter is my world. The very breath in my lungs. I would move heaven and earth for her to have a full life. Fifty percent is too big a risk. St. Andrews is working on a drug to prevent the disease. The other hospital is developing a treatment. Your sister and the other patients were never going to get better at St. Andrews."

Rage boiled through me. Her last moments haunted me, clinging to hope. Believing in the treatment. In the doctors. In me. What would she say if she saw me now, trapped and helpless? Would she be proud of me for getting this far or angry that I hadn't done more? My fists clenched in my mind, useless against the weight pinning me down. I wanted to lunge at the woman in front of me, scream until the walls shattered. But all I could do was burn... burn with hatred for this woman.

She got up and walked toward the door. "Don't worry. Dr. Suleman will take care of everything." After smoothing her hair again, she rested her hand on the doorknob. "Our friend Yacena will ensure you disappear. Killing two birds with one stone. We did some creative editing. Made it look like Mr. Bishop picked you up. So your disappearance will be pinned on him."

She turned back toward me. Tears spilled from my eyes, not just from grief but from the crushing weight of betrayal. And now, I might not live long enough to make it right.

Fear wrapped around my chest, the thought of them pinning my murder on Alejandro made me want to claw out her eyes.

I hated this helplessness. Lying here, unable to move. I could only pray that Alejandro was hearing all of this. That the device worked. But how long did it last? There was no way to know if he'd received the last message, let alone this confession. Every second stretched like a lifetime.

"Don't cry. But wouldn't you agree? My plan is quite genius."

She undid the safety lock and pulled open the door. Surprise flared across her face as Dr. Suleman stumbled into the room.

Fifty-Eight

Bishop

As I drove to the hotel, my heart pounded, a tight pressure building in my chest. Adrenaline surged through my limbs, sharp and hot. Instinct screamed that something didn't add up. When I called the hotel, they said the group from the conference room left at least forty minutes ago. But Elena's tracker hadn't moved.

She wouldn't have lost it. If something happened to it, she would've told me. And this was the second hour with no check-in. Her security still didn't answer his phone.

I jumped out of the vehicle, tossed my keys to the valet, and rushed to the reception desk.

"This is urgent. Can you please point me to the conference room?"

The receptionist looked up, tucking a strand of hair behind her ear as her lips curved into a lazy smile. She didn't rush or flinch at my urgency. She blinked, slow and smooth, her gaze drifting over me, clocking every inch of my six-foot-two frame. Then she leaned back in the chair, drinking me in like she didn't care if Monday came on Thursday.

"They forget something again? Guess you're not part of the team. Are you, like, one of their assistants?"

"You could say that."

She pointed me down a path past the swimming pool, toward the back of the property near the golf course. As I followed the route, I prayed for noise, movement, anything to lead me to her.

The conference room sat in silence. Coffee cups cluttered the table, the bitter scent of overbrewed coffee hung in the air. On the side table, bits of cake and half-eaten sandwiches remained, alongside sliced fruit slumped in their own juices. The smell of sugar and wilted greens mingled with the cool sterility of air conditioning. Then, as I turned to leave, a muffled voice rose from behind the podium.

I moved slowly to the front of the room. The hum grew louder, pressing in. My hand skimmed the wall until it bumped into something cool and metallic near the top of the door. A catch. Probably a hidden button nearby, but I didn't have time to search. I wedged my fingers into the seam and forced it open.

Elena's bodyguard was bound and gagged inside, slumped in the dim glow of a single emergency light. The air reeked of sweat and confinement, stale and heavy, suffocating. His breathing came shallow, eyes blinking as though waking from a nightmare. Using my back to prop the door open, I pulled him out. His face flushed, wrists marked from struggling against the restraints. I took out my switchblade and cut the rope around his feet.

"What—" Before I could form my question he responded.

"They gave me coffee," he said. "That part I can remember. Next thing, I woke up in blackness."

They couldn't have taken Elena out through the lobby. Her tracker still pinged strong. She was here.

"Sorry, man. I messed up."

"We need to find her." Years of training held me back from tearing the place apart. That and the risk of getting her killed.

"They couldn't have gone far. Do you know where the team is staying?"

"After lunch, they went toward the villas near the golf course."

That made sense. Remote. Quiet. Hidden from prying eyes.

But which villa?

I pulled out my phone. It took ten seconds to piggyback off the conference room's unsecured Wi-Fi. Another five seconds I couldn't afford, but I used them to inject a silent query into the hotel's internal system.

My watch vibrated. Her voice cracked through it, faint and slurred. *"H'llooo."* The sound jolted through me, slicing clean past logic and training. Relief surged, sharp and immediate, but it had no time to settle before panic slammed into me.

She was alive. I pictured her teasing smile, the spark in her eyes. I was not losing her. Not today.

I hit record. A refined cultured voice cut in. The woman responded to Elena's fragment of slurred questions, clearly not knowing that she was being recorded.

I pulled up the list of villas rented under the construction company's name. One stood out: Villa 6, under Dr. Suleman.

"Let's go. I know where they have her."

We rushed toward the villas while someone strode a parallel path. A man with a haversack. I recognized him instantly. "Dr. Suleman on your right," I murmured to the bodyguard.

I veered toward him, as if by chance, crossing paths, but the bodyguard kept walking straight

When I bumped into Dr. Suleman, I leaned in. "If you try to scream or shout," I said in a calm, icy whisper, pressing my gun into him, "this bullet will pierce your spleen and detonate your internal organs."

The color drained from his face, leaving it pale and stiff like carved marble.

"Who ... who are you? What do ... what do you want?"

"You have something precious that belongs to me." A bead of sweat broke on his upper lip. "I'm here to take her back. Keep walking."

His silence told me everything. His mouth flattened, not quite anger, not quite regret, the expression of a man who'd run out of excuses. He'd taken something. Now he either showed me where Elana was, or I'd rip it out of him. His choice.

Fifty-Nine

Bishop

"*Dr. Suleman will take care of everything ...*" Elizabeth Wakefield rambled from Elena's recording device as she waited for the good doctor. Her voice amplified the unease already crawling beneath my skin, each word grating like nails on glass. The entire operation was her deluded brainchild. Everyone else? Mere pawns.

I handed Elena's bodyguard my phone to call the police and kept my gun pressed to Dr. Suleman's ribs. One wrong move, and I wouldn't hesitate. As we reached the door, I told him, "Easy. Pull out the card and swipe."

He swiped and pushed just as the door pulled from the other side. The sudden give threw off his balance, and he stumbled forward, catching himself against the doorframe before he could hit the floor. My gun shifted, now aimed at Elizabeth Wakefield. Her face twisted in shock, her eyes wide, darting across the room. A cold, tight knot coiled in my stomach at the sight, part disbelief, part satisfaction. For a heartbeat, I almost pitied her. Almost. She blinked rapidly, as if trying to clear a fog. I kept my gaze locked on her.

Hurting a woman never crossed my mind, until this moment. I wanted to kill her with my bare hands when I saw Elena's tear-streaked face. How she laid on the bed helplessly, the needle in her vein prepped for an IV.

"Tell me, why I shouldn't kill you right now?" I stared at her, hoping that she could sense my hatred and disgust.

The bodyguard approached Elena.

Elizabeth snapped. "No. No. You brought them here. All my years of planning!"

She whirled toward Dr. Suleman. "If you don't do something, your daughter will go to jail and never see the light of day. I'll make sure of it."

At the mention of his daughter, his face flushed dark. His jaw clenched so tight a muscle jumped near his temple. He didn't blink. His shoulders stiffened; hands curled into fists at his sides.

"What do you want me to do, Elizabeth?" he shot back. "You think I could give you the syringe or hook up an IV while he's pointing a gun at us? He'd shoot us both." Letting out a breath, his shoulders sagged, removing some invisible weight that rested on them. He said, "It's over Elizabeth."

She held something over him. Something personal.

Her lips curled with venom, like a serpent ready to strike. "Over. Never."

I kept my weapon trained on Elizabeth.

Elizabeth sneered, her voice low and laced with icy triumph. "Your precious daughter will never follow in your footsteps... all because someone found white powder in her suitcase." She stood rigid, chin high, as if daring anyone to challenge her, her presence thickening the already charged air.

She spat, "You spineless fool. Always weak. I offered you everything, money, a shot at being a Nobel laureate. You needed a little incentive... your poor daughter."

It all happened in slow motion. Dr. Suleman lunged with a guttural cry, slamming her onto the carpet with a thud that rattled the room. Her scream ripped through the air, high-pitched, frantic, raw.

He jammed a hand into his pants pocket and wrestled out a capped syringe. His fingers shook as he yanked the cap free and drove the needle into her neck. She shrieked again, more in disbelief than pain. Blood speckled his hand, but he didn't flinch.

"Rot in hell," he growled, leaving the blood where it had landed on his now trembling hand.

Sixty

Elena

When Dr. Suleman stumbled into the room, I thought my final moments were coming. I was going to take my last breaths, not surrounded by people who loved me but by those who plotted my demise.

With my nightmarish ordeal over, and after a few hours of observation, they finally discharged me. If I never saw another hospital again, I'd be happy. Alejandro wheeled me to the car himself, refusing to let the orderly help. The early morning air hit my skin, cool and crisp, carrying the faint scent of antiseptic and car exhaust as we pushed through the doors. I welcomed it like a promise of freedom. I longed to board a plane and fly straight to Miami, but the police asked us to stay at least two more days.

Imani and Pastor Jonas, *Dad*, were already on their way. It wouldn't surprise me if they were waiting at the house when we arrived.

Alejandro rested his hand on my shoulder. He was steady, warm, comforting. Home.

When he walked into that room, God answered a prayer I didn't dare to speak: *You'll get married. You'll grow old.*

The thought barely settled before fear clawed up my throat. For a split second, I thought, *What if they turned on him instead?* But when my bodyguard followed them in, he rushed to my side and whispered an apology. Then I rested easier.

Everything unraveled quickly from there. The confrontation left Elizabeth Wakefield sedated in a hospital bed, the poison still infiltrating her system. A drug designed to save lives, twisted into something deadly.

Alejandro lifted me from the wheelchair and eased me into the front seat. My legs trembled, weak and tingling with pinpricks that burned like tiny sparks of fire racing beneath my skin. Nausea churned low in my belly, and the world tilted slightly as dizziness swept over me. The drugs weren't fully out of my system yet. It would take days.

As he pulled out of the parking lot, he rested his hand on my thigh. "You're quiet."

The dark sky held the hush of dawn, that sacred hour before light breaks through. A faint orange glow kissed the horizon, and somewhere in the distance, a lone bird stirred, its song soft but certain, like the world exhaling after holding its breath all night.

I covered Alejandro's hand with mine, letting the touch speak love, trust, and everything words couldn't express.

Turning my hand and linking our fingers, he told me, "Terror gripped me. My mind kept whispering, 'You're not going to get to her in time.'"

"But you did." My voice caught. "You saved me."

"I wish I had figured it out sooner. When I dug into the ownership of the shell companies behind the two pharmaceutical firms, everything pointed to Wakefield Corporation. It was almost genius. She held controlling interest in both competing companies, Nano Health Care and DaCosta Biopharma."

I laced my fingers through his. "Dr. Suleman ... he was a reluctant monster. Elizabeth Wakefield destroyed so many lives ... just trying to save one."

"And now she's going to lose hers," he whispered.

The blur of trees and buildings rushed past the window. Lord, I longed for my bed. To be home. To hopefully put all of this behind me. I tightened my hold on Alejandro's hand. With the police and the ongoing investigation, it would be weeks, even months before we saw the end of all of this. In Miami, the police had already taken Yacena into custody. Justice had started to turn its wheels.

I couldn't save Zoë or Kellie ... but I'm certain there are many others we were able to save by exposing this evil, twisted plot.

The hospice was never for care. It was her trial ground. Victims masked as patients, dying under the illusion of love and comfort. They would have no idea they were nothing more than test rats. Stripped of their human right to spend their final days with dignity. Dr. Suleman, overcome with grief and sorrow, shared it all with the police.

Our hands stayed linked.

The last few hours taught me the danger of twisted love. It masqueraded as sacrifice but left only ruin in its wake.

As much as I didn't want to feel anything but hatred for her … I did.

In a few hours, she'd take her final breath.

Sixty-One

Elena

With the danger finally behind us, Dad and I returned home last week. Zen and Alejandro made sure we had state-of-the-art security, including a guard stationed at the entrance of the gated community from nine at night until seven in the morning.

Dad agreed to Zen demolishing Zoë's home and using both plots to build a large family house, a place where we could gather for events. I expected him to refuse. I even braced myself for the shake of his head, the sorrow in his eyes, the inability to let the last of her go. But he surprised me. My breath caught when he said, *"Zoë's memories didn't live in her house. They live in my heart."* Warmth surged in my chest, the kind that made my throat tight and my eyes sting. I hadn't expected that from him, not so soon.

Alejandro slipped into the seat beside me. The worship team asked us to stand, their voices rising as they led us into the praise and worship session. When they finished, Dad J stepped forward.

Calling just one of them "Dad" didn't feel right. Dad J and Dad T felt right. Both mattered to me.

As the worship team exited the stage, Dad J took the microphone. "Today's sermon is about second chances. More specifically my second chance."

If a feather dropped in the last row, we would've heard it from where we sat in the third.

Dad J spoke of a love that slipped away. The mistakes he and Imani had made. How they found their way back to each other, to service, to faith. Before the service, they asked if it was okay to tell the congregation about me, and we agreed.

Dad J stood tall. His voice rang out, though it cracked now and then. "God gave me a second chance with a girl I loved. She blossomed into a beautiful woman. Imani."

Gasps and soft murmurs floated through the church.

Imani stepped forward in a flowing orange dress. She took his hand.

"We were young," she said. "We made a mistake. I paid the price. We had a daughter I never mentioned to him. My family moved away, and the child was eventually placed for adoption." She glanced at me, then back at him.

Dad J continued. "That too became a second chance. Because God gave me back the woman I've loved since I was seventeen.

And a daughter I've watched over spiritually for the last few years. Now, I get to share her with her other father. She likes to say God blessed her with two dads and two moms."

I stood, my knees shaky, heart pounding like a drum in my chest. I squeezed Dad T's hand, his grip steady and centering, then took a breath and walked toward my biological parents. My throat ached with emotion, but I held my head high and joined them at the front. Dad J reached for me.

"God gave us a second chance to be a family. An extended one."

My adoptive father then stepped up beside us. Then Alejandro.

Dad J turned to the congregation. "I hope you can see our love, look past our pasts, and still accept me as your pastor."

The entire church stood. Applause thundered around us. A lump rose in my throat as people came forward, some with tears in their eyes. One by one, they embraced us like we already belonged.

Dad J didn't have to do this. He didn't have to lead this church. But he did. Because this was his true calling.

My fingers found Alejandro's, his hand warm around mine. Facing your fears didn't erase them, but it sure made space for miracles.

Sixty-Two

Bishop

This was my tenth consecutive Sunday at church. It started the day I came to support Jonas when he and Imani stood before the congregation declaring their love for each other. I never meant to keep coming. But something pulled me back, week after week, without anyone asking.

I even downloaded a Bible app. Got ambitious and signed up for a ninety-day reading plan for the four Gospels. Finished it last week, with days to spare. I talked to Jonas almost every day during that time. Not once did he grow impatient with my questions, arguments, or even my outright skepticism.

Elena stepped onto the platform with her mom, bathed in the warm glow of the overhead lights that cast soft shadows on the polished wood floor. The first gentle chords of "I Surrender All" drifted through the sanctuary, tender and haunting. Elena's face held a calm, almost reverent focus, while her mother's expression shimmered with emotion, eyes glistening as if holding back tears.

My parents and sister were always religious. But for the first time, as the music washed over me, something shifted, like a lock turning inside my chest. A sudden peace spread through me, unexpected and almost uncomfortable, as if some part of me I had sealed off now stirred awake.

I knew about God, but I didn't know Him. Not like they did. Not like Elena did.

What did it even mean to surrender all of yourself? What would that look like for someone like me, with the kind of work I did? People like us don't retire peacefully in the suburbs. Some of the people we take out need to be removed. But where did that leave me? Could I fit into something like this? Could God accept me truly?

Surely my soul was not too black for Jesus to want me.

As the music faded, Jonas stepped forward. "Surrendering all to Jesus; what does that look like? In our humanness, we want to figure it all out before we trust Him. But there's no person He can't reach. No soul He's not interested in."

I froze. Could he hear me from here?

"There's no soul too dark for Him. He wants you, as you are. As the song plays again, if you want to trust Jesus and surrender all, raise your hand. Right where you are. I'll pray for you."

The music swelled again. He couldn't mean me. Could he? A voice inside whispered, *"Not you."* I almost believed it.

How would this work, God? There's so much blood on my hands. Thick, clinging guilt seeped into every crevice of my mind, staining everything I touched.

The music dipped, softer now.

"Is there anyone else who wants to surrender all today?" Pastor Jonas's voice cut through everything. "Stop trying to figure it out. Just let the Lord lead you."

As Pastor Jonas began to pray, a tremor started in my fingers. My chest tightened. My heartbeat thudded in my ears, louder than the music. My hand lifted, slow, hesitant, but sure. Before I could talk myself out of it, I raised my hand.

Maybe ... just maybe my soul could be saved after all.

Epilogue

Bishop

Six Months Later

"My gosh, why did I share my secret with you? But I do love playing tourist," Elena bubbled as we allowed the driver to scan our tickets.

I guided her to a seat and handed her headphones. Leaning in, I teased, "You probably could recite everything they'll say."

"Part of the fun is listening to it with fresh ears and through the eyes of a tourist," she added, slipping on the earphones and putting up a finger in a silent *hush*.

I shook my head. We got off at Lincoln Mall. The warm afternoon sun kissed our skin as we strolled hand in hand toward the spot where we had the sketch done by the artist. The scent of roasted almonds drifted through the air, blending with the faint hum of music and conversation.

"I hope he's here to capture our second trip, now that I've fully converted you to playing tourist," she said, smiling at me.

We stopped and shared a cone, the cold strawberry-chocolate twist soft serve melting fast in the heat, the sticky sweetness clinging to our fingers.

"You want to get off at Wynwood or Little Havana?" I asked, tucking a wayward strand of hair behind her ear.

Her smile tempted me. I leaned forward and brushed her sticky lips with mine.

"Strawberry-chocolate ice cream tastes even better from your lips," she said as her tongue darted over her bottom lip.

Color warmed her cheeks. "Are you blushing?"

"Shush. And both ... I want to visit both," she finally answered.

We walked back toward the stop to meet the bus. Unlike the last time, we didn't unlink our hands. Elena is the one constant in my life. With her, everything feels easier. Loving her wasn't complicated. It was as natural as breathing.

I'd never loved someone as purely as I have Elena. We've kissed, oh boy, we've kissed, and my body responded to her every touch with a deep desire. But have I wanted to take it further? For the first time in my life, no.

She wanted to wait until marriage. I could wait. For her.

We stayed on the bus until our stop, then got off at Wynwood and entered the first section. A gate blocked access to the paid area.

Bumping my shoulder, she frowned. "We can't go in. Maybe there's a celebrity or a movie shoot going on."

She turned to leave, but I kept our hands linked. "Let me see what I can do."

I approached one of the workers, we spoke quietly, and he opened the gate.

Inside, a tent with a table sat in the center of the courtyard. Soft white fabric draped from the ceiling. Flowers ran down the middle of the table, and polished glass reflected hints of sunlight. The faint aroma of jasmine lingered in the air. As we stepped through the gates and walked toward the tent's opening, Elena froze beside me. Her eyes locked on the people inside. Her lips parted slightly. She blinked, then again, slower this time, as if her mind struggled to catch up. Her hand rose to her chest, fingers curling.

Inside the tent sat our parents, Zeno, Drago, Aimee, Jaden, and his wife Tanisha.

A flute played softly in the background.

I dropped to both knees. "I told you when I proposed, it wouldn't be on one knee, but both. Elena Callos, will you spend the rest of your life with me?"

"Yes!" she offered without hesitation. "Alejandro Bishop, I will spend the rest of my life with you."

I slipped an emerald ring with a halo of diamonds onto her finger. She knelt to meet me, and we kissed. Nearby, the artist sat with his sketchpad, eyes focused, pencil moving steadily across the page. He captured our first perfect day months ago on

Lincoln Road. I prayed he captured all the love in this moment too, two souls kneeling in love and surrender.

Two Years Later

Elena

"Aimee, have you heard anything?" My chest tightened. Drago and Alejandro were on a mission in South America to take out the head of a cartel, but no one had heard from them in two days. Jaden and Leila, supporting them from base, confirmed they'd lost all contact with them.

I rested my hand on the small bump. Five months in, and I was barely showing. God, please bring them home safely. Alejandro expressed concerns about this mission, but the pressure to remove the cartel leader was necessary for political stability in that region. It was one of those 'cut off the head and the body will die' operations.

Both my dads and Imani came over. Following Zen's example, Alejandro demolished my old house and built a new one. A home he promised to fill with love and laughter and many children. I loved that I still lived close to Dad.

Mom brought out tea and coffee for everyone. I couldn't do this. Since we'd been married, this was the most dangerous assignment Alejandro had accepted. I couldn't lose him. I wanted our child to grow up with both parents.

Around midnight, everyone left for their homes. I promised to call if I heard anything. I curled up on the sofa, its cushions warm and comforting beneath me. Silence pressed against my chest, thick and heavy, broken only by the ticking clock and my uneven breathing. Sleeping in our bed wasn't an option. Too many memories. His scent still lingered, bringing both comfort and worry.

A sharp trill of the phone pierced the darkness, jolting me upright. I reached for it on the side table next to the sofa, my heart hammering as I saw the time: 2:36 a.m.

I took a breath before answering.

"Babe?"

His voice never sounded better. Tears of relief and joy rushed to my eyes.

"Alejandro? God, I thought I'd never hear your voice again. Drago? Are you both okay?"

"Someone double-crossed us. They leaked our location. We finished the job, but all hell broke loose afterward. Then, by some miracle, a man and his daughter showed up and gave us cover to escape."

"Where are you?"

"In Peru. We're boarding the plane now. Drago's talking to Aimee. He took a bullet in the shoulder."

"You?"

"Just a graze to my side."

"I love you. Thank you, God, for keeping him safe. When you get home, we're going to talk about this job. I don't plan to raise our child alone."

"You want to know what kept me determined to live when all those shots were firing at us? I thought of all the ways I still have yet to show you how much I love you."

"You sure you didn't bump your head?" I laughed.

"When I get home, know that I'm going to make up for all the stress I put you through. I'm going to kiss you from your head to toe and every place in between."

"Alejandro," I moaned as heat rushed over me. Baby hormones made me hot and bothered. "You better keep your promise."

"I always do, babe. I always do."

Five Years Later

Bishop

Elena's family filled the entire fourth row, center stage at Cadogan Hall. Over the last five years, she had accepted more invitations to perform outside of church, but this marked the first time she said yes to playing with an orchestra. The music director had called while we were having dinner. Her gaze slid to our two children, eyes full of quiet resolve, and she said yes without hesitation.

Later that night, curled beside me as we lay talking after making love, her finger traced a slow line down my chest. Then, as if sharing a long-held secret, she whispered, "I said yes tonight because I want our children to believe they can do anything." She wanted them to see that sometimes, in life, we have to face our fears and overcome them.

After three months of practice, here we were in London, all of us gathered to support this woman. The one who was the glue that brought this extended family together.

Imani sat next to me with her granddaughter in her lap, the little one freshly two and full of curiosity. Even Zeno took a break from conquering the world to be here.

The curtain parted. The orchestra sat ready on stage. The conductor marched out and bowed. Then Elena stepped forward, the lights catching the faint shimmer of her earrings, the ones I gave her when we celebrated her first birthday together. After all these years, she was rarely without them.

She wore black. Simple. Elegant. Her eyes didn't search the crowd. She didn't need to. She belonged to the music now. Her fingers flexed slightly before lifting the flute.

Cadogan Hall held its breath.

The conductor raised his hands. Silence deepened.

Then she played.

And God, she was beautiful.

She stood there, in front of hundreds, in a foreign city, and she played.

For them.

For us.

For herself.

Ten Years Later

I pulled up the file on the tablet. My next client was twenty-three years old. This would be the first of many visits. For at least the next ten years, we would share a professional relationship. Her blood work showed normal levels. But the genetic panel told a different story. She carried a mutation that increased her risk for pancreatic cancer.

I tapped the button on my desk. "Karen, please send in Miss Wakefield."

The door opened and she stepped in. Her hazel eyes met mine. I stood, walked around the desk, and offered my hand.

"I'm Dr. Suleman. Please have a seat."

Olivia Wakefield sat. Although it was our first meeting, I already knew far more about her than she could possibly imagine. Not because of who she was, but because of who her grandmother had been.

As her grandmother lay dying, my father had given her a choice. Confess to planting the drugs in my suitcase, or he would withhold his research. At the time, he was close to perfecting the treatment.

In her final breaths, Elizabeth Wakefield placed her granddaughter's future above her own reputation.

Elizabeth Wakefield ruined so many lives. In some ways, she ruined mine too. I changed after that entire ordeal. Anyone would have... I never trusted people the same way again.

My father's medical license had been suspended. But he worked beside me, quietly and faithfully, helping bring the life-saving drug to market. It became his redemption.

Olivia Wakefield didn't know me. Not really.

But how ironic that the woman her grandmother tried to destroy was the same one who would now walk this journey with her. And, if the time ever came, might be the one to save her life.

Life has a way of circling back.

Blurb

They say love changes a man. I wasn't looking to change.

I should've minded my own business. Tuned her out. Kept my eye on the passing numbers.

After all, the elevator was meant for one...me.

But she was there. On her phone. In my elevator. So, I listened.

What started as idle curiosity turned into concern. Then it got messy.

Now I'm neck-deep in something darker than I bargained for. And someone's trying to silence her before I even figure out if she's my salvation or my undoing.

Elena Callos wasn't my type. Or so I thought.

The thing is, I'm Alejandro Bishop. And I don't lose what matters to me.

Elena Callos... matters.

From My Heart to Yours

Even the strongest women need someone to lean on, whether that is family, friends, or the man we will one day marry. I hope Bishop and Elena's journey reminded you that love and strength can walk hand in hand.

N. R. Emerald

HAPPY READING!